A BIT OFF THE MAP
and other stories

A BIT OFF THE MAP

and other stories

by

ANGUS WILSON

London : SECKER & WARBURG : 1957

FOR FRANCIS AND HONORIA

Printed in England
at The Windmill Press
Kingswood, Surrey
and
first published 1957
by
Martin Secker & Warburg Ltd
7 John Street, London
*W.C.*1.

Contents

A Bit off the Map

SEE, some people go about like it doesn't matter why we're here or what it's all for, but I'm not like that. I want to get at the Truth. Of course, it's not easy because there's a lot that think they know, but even if they do, they're not telling anyone else. Same as it might be with the Government. A lot's secret and we can't tell what they're doing. But about this other truth—the important one—like what the religions pretend to know, I think it's more of a question of keeping on worrying at it and making up your mind that you'll find out. At least that's how I see it. And now I've met Huggett and The Crowd, I'm likely to be lucky—because Huggett's a sort of philosopher and a mystic too. Only like me he's quite young.

They've sent me a parcel for my birthday. But I won't go back there. Not unless I was to go back and perhaps kill her, see; and I might do because I don't know my own strength. I'm not very tall, just average, but I'm well made all right. I could go for a model if I wanted. There's crowds of artists have asked me—sometimes it's just funny stuff, of course, but mostly it's genuine. They'd be glad to get me because, I've got proportions; not just health and strength stuff—muscles and that just goes to fat. Well paid too, but you've got to be able to take it, because it's tiring work modelling, I could do it though if I wanted; I don't know my own strength. I wouldn't take a job like that though, because maybe I'll be an artist and then it'd be bad if I'd been a model. At least that's how I see it. You never hear of models becoming artists. Models are usually just layabouts.

It could be I *might* be a painter too. I've got an eye for colours. But I haven't found myself yet. That's what I've got to do now—find what's really there, what really goes to make up the being they call Kennie Martin. (It's all right, too, I can tell you—not just the physique like what I said already but the eyes and the mouth. If I use them most times I can get anything I want.) "Being they call Kennie Martin" that's like they put it in novels, see, it's more subtle. I notice things like that. That's why it might be I might be a writer. But I've got to find myself first. And that means going deep down. Of course, a lot of it's sex. I can get most what I want but I don't know what I want. See, it's like I read "the personality is a delicate balance between mind and body. In each personality the balance between male and female is delicate too" or something like that. That was in a book I bought second-hand—*The Balance of Being* by James T. Whiteway. Or it might have been Havelock Ellis, because I've read that too—cases and all. But I know all that anyway. Like you get a woman that fancies you but then she won't let you have it unless you're wearing a special sort of belt or socks or something. Or like it might be a queer that dresses up as a maid. I know it all, but I won't say whether I know it personally or not. I never admit. That's one thing you learn in the life I lead—never admit anything. Let the other man do the talking and if there's questions you don't like, just stare. Only you must put all the power you've got into it. It's a matter of Will Power—one or the other of you goes down. With me, the other man goes down. So I don't say what I know from experience—not in detail, that is.

Lots of times I don't work because the jobs they offer don't take you any place worth going or because like now I've got to be free until I find myself. Well, I've got to sleep somewhere, haven't I? That's all I'm saying. (If you answer like that and smile a bit sideways, it makes people interested—it's a mystery, see, and everyone's a sucker for a mystery.) But personal or not, I know all the prostitutes and the ponces and that. I shan't get stuck there, because I've something big in me that'll take me to the top when I find myself.

All the same it's a world that keeps you on your toes, because you've got to think and talk quick in that world. I mean like a prostitute's got to think and act quick if she's to live. Anyhow I've read it, too, how criminals and artists are all together; see, they've got to be, because society's ranged against them. It was in *Picture Post* one week about it. Like Rimbaud. There was a bloke lived in Fulham who read some of Rimbaud's poems to me. Souls of the Damned or something, because art means you have to suffer. Huggett says Rimbaud found out about himself and then he quit. Went out for big money and made it. Slave trade or something. Lots of artists are sadists, see. But Huggett says he wasn't any good anyway. He says real genius means Will Power. All this art and suffering is just cock, Huggett says. (I don't like

it when Huggett uses those words—cock and that. A lot
of these intellectuals talk like that, "C—— this and, f——
that"—but all as though the words would bite them. I
just stare at them when they talk like that. They soon
stop. But Huggett isn't like that. When he speaks he
means it. All the same he uses the words—cock and all
that. I don't know why.) Well, anyway Rimbaud once
was sitting in a café—with the poets and all, queers a lot
of them, the bloke who told me was queer himself. And
he suddenly lashed out with a knife and cut the fingers of
these others. On the table.

That's what I've done. I suddenly see red, especially if
someone's done me a wrong thing. I don't forgive, I
don't believe in that. I half killed another boy at school.
That's what got me into trouble first. There's four or
five people in the world that I'd like to cut the guts out
of. I often think of that. It's like I said about my step-
mother. If I went back there I'm liable to half kill her,
because I might see red and I don't know my own
strength. So it's no good their sending me birthday
presents. They're all earning good money there now but
all they sent me's five pounds. Not that I blame them.
All the same a lot of that's going on what they wouldn't
like. Haircut and that. And a bottle of good stuff—it
doesn't dry the hair, see, because if you put spirit on it it's
liable to crack; and it gives colour without any dye.
Pour les hommes, it's called.

Well, as I say, they don't believe in me. They think
I'm just a layabout or worse. But I don't worry. They'll
see. I'm just finding myself, that's all. If my mother
hadn't died, she'd have understood. She saw to it that I

speak well, because, see, I speak good English, but I can't write very easy. Of course, if I turned out to be a poet, that'd be different, because there it isn't writing, it's the words, like they have to have power. Poetry's like painting in words. That's how I see it. She took me to see the psychologist, because I'd seen red and half killed that boy. But then she died and *he* didn't see any good to psychologists. And then he married this bitch. The psychologist said I'd got to find myself, at least I think he did. I don't remember very well. All the same I had a low I.Q. and that was the same in the army. I used to worry about that, but Huggett says all that's cock. And the same about that I didn't do very well at school.

Look, I'm trying to find out what it's all about. Because when you look at it, it doesn't seem very much good. But I've always known it did mean something—life and all I mean. Not religion, mind you. I used to think that and I went to a lot of these churches. Because he and my step-mother didn't bother about that. A car and old time dancing and the pictures. That's about all they think of —and sex, of course. I see red when I think of that. Chris, that's their son, has been given a Lambretta because he's got a grant to Teachers' Training College. I don't say I wish he'd kill himself on it, but pretty near. Well, any-way, with them not believing in religion and that, I used to think there must be something to it. My mother always went Christmas and Easter. (I wonder sometimes if there wasn't something funny about who my father was. I'd like to get at the truth of who I really am. I know my mother never wanted to have it with him. I wouldn't blame her even if it was someone else. I'd be

glad although it'd mean giving myself an ugly name.
Also it would account for a lot, like why I'm different.)
So I went to all the churches—there's lots nobody knows
much about like The Church of the Latter Day Saints and
that. And I listened at Marble Arch. But I didn't find
what I wanted. Like it's what Huggett says they've only
got a part and they make out it's the whole. It stands to
reason there must be a whole Truth somewhere. Anyway what they said didn't seem to go along the way I was
looking. See it's like I say when I want to give someone
the brush off—"I don't fancy anything with you, thanks
all the same". There was more in a book I bought once—
A Triangle of Light. An analysis of mysticism, by J. G. Partridge, D.Litt. What I got through of it, that is. It gave,
see, the Inner Meaning. But Huggett says he's never
heard of the book and he doesn't go much for the idea of
it, maybe it wasn't much—see, I was only seventeen when
I bought that book.

Huggett's writing a book that's to go a long way for
finding out the Truth, but it'll take him years to write
because it's not only religion he's taking in but philosophy. So he works in this shipping office, but he has
poems published and he's got all these followers—The
Crowd they're called. Truth and Reality—it's thousands
of years men have been searching for it. What's real?—
Aristotle said it was what we see, and Plato said it was
what we couldn't see, like what's behind things. I read
about that in a digest. And Socrates said Know Thyself.
But Huggett says that it's more the Will. We've got to
breed a new race with real Will Power. It's Will Power
that'll get you to the top too.

Of course I could get jobs with prospects, but what's it mean? There they go, like I see them on the tubes and buses and maybe they'll have a house in the suburbs and a car and a wife and kids, and mostly when they've got these, they drop dead. Don't be an anonymous man, Huggett says. That's what he calls them. We're in a hurry, my generation. And anyway I've got to have time to think and to find myself. So mostly I take short jobs like loading things on vans (but I'm not very strong) and doorman and working in the ice-cream factory and waiter. And mostly I change rooms. We're restless, we're in a hurry. And sometimes I just sleep around where I can find it, but, like, well it's not always to my taste, though it's company and I get lonely on my own. But still you've got to have the will to stand alone if you are going to get anywhere. Sometimes I've got a room of my own *and* I'm between jobs like now and that's the best.

Of course, maybe success might come sudden, like I saw a map the other day showing all the buried treasure that's been found in England (I don't know much of the country, except the approved school was in Yorkshire on the moors) or there's unclaimed moneys, you can get a list of them if you ask for it. I've got the figure and legs that could make a dancer and I could sing, if only I could stop smoking. There's Elvis Presley's got all these cars and Tommy Steele started just in a skiffle group like in one of the coffee bars that I spend most time in. (You have to learn to make one coffee last.) Look at Carroll Levis's discoveries, those are all young, but that's not serious. Traditional's more serious. But in any case, I don't go

much for dreaming like that, because see you've got to
keep your wits about you if you're going to think about
the Truth, and it's most only layabouts that dream of
making millions on pools or like perhaps being England's
Johnnie Ray overnight.

All the same it was chance that I met The Crowd.
Susan's a school teacher. We got talking in the Italian
coffee house and she was the girl friend then of Reg that's
the next to Huggett. I think he'd like to be the principal
himself, but Huggett's a genius and he's not. And Reg
believes in Power and what he says is Shit in the face of
humanity—if millions have to be liquidated what's it
matter? most people are never alive anyway but Huggett
believes in Power and Leadership for the Regenerations
of the World. So they often quarrel. At first Reg didn't
like for me to be there because it was obvious I appealed
to Susan, but now he's with this other girl Rosa, see, who
works as a typist. Reg doesn't work much himself. And
then, see, they mostly (the men, that is) dress very badly
—dirty old flannel trousers, I wouldn't think to wear, and
coats (who wear coats?) and they don't have their hair
cut anywhere good, if at all—partly it's they're too busy
thinking and talking, partly it's they don't like anything
that might look queer, mostly it's they don't like anything that looks bourgeois (only Huggett tells Susan not
to be a fool when she calls a thing bourgeois). Well, me
being dressed as I am—see, when I've got money I buy
my jeans and sweaters at this place where they make
specially for you (so you never see the same on anyone
else) and my hair cut at Raymond 15/- with Pour les
Hommes, and my jeans very tight because I've got good

legs. Well, see, The Crowd thought I might be on to some game (but what have they got to lose?) or a queer (The Crowd is strong against queers, but Susan could tell them different about me) or in with a teddy boy lot (but I'm always alone). So they didn't act very friendly at first (except Susan—and the women, in The Crowd, they don't count too much) but I thought, as it might well be I'd be an artist or a writer, this was my chance (because even Huggett says in England the world of artists and writers is very tough to make, you've got to smash your way through) and then what they talked about is what I want to hear—see, about Truth and Will Power and Genius—and especially Huggett; and I get very lonely. So when I was with Susan and we were with The Crowd, I didn't speak, I just listened. That's another trick, if you want something or somebody, don't say anything, it seems like a mystery, see, which as I say people like. Also The Crowd, even Huggett, like listeners. But mostly anyway I wanted to listen—it was what I must hear if I'm to find myself—and, see, I haven't had much education so I have to listen hard. At first, I don't think Huggett noticed me. Then one day Reg started that there probably wasn't any Reason for it, any Truth about it, just being smarter than the next man. That made Huggett mad with him. So I said what Reg said couldn't be right, because it stood to reason there was the Truth to find somewhere. And after that Huggett started to ask for me when I wasn't there and told Susan to bring me along. So now I go with them mostly. (And about being lonely—that's what I tell when someone's interested in me. I know how to do it all—about my mother being dead and that bitch my step-mother, and whether perhaps he's not my father at all. And mostly it gets them—sometimes they say, "Look take this couple of pounds and nothing asked in return." I tell it big-eyed and lost because I could be an actor, maybe I will when I find myself. But what's funny is it's true. I don't think too much about it because you have to be on your own and be tough. So it's like I'm shooting a line and it's true all the same which is funny really.) But The Crowd's not the same as the Angry young men which you read about. Someone said it was and Huggett got very angry, because it's by Love and Leadership that the Will works. And all these angry young men believe in democracy and freedom and a lot of stuff that Huggett says just gets in the way of real thinking.

All the same The Crowd *is* angry because what's being done and written now is all cock. Huggett says it's only time before their ideas come to the top, but, all the same, like I said, our generation is in a hurry. And I get angry, too, like I said, so that I could kill them all—the foremen and the headwaiters and the police and the girls that want to be kind and the queers that want to be kind and him writing from Southampton. "You know, Kennie, and I've told you often and again there's a bed for you here and jobs too if you treat your step-mother right and don't mix with the rotten crowd off the ships that you did when you were here. For they are a rotten crowd, Kennie, you know. And you mustn't think we don't want you." I don't *think* about that, I *know*. The bitch worked to get me out and I'm not going back unless if I go back as something big that she'll have to listen to. But I mustn't

think about it too much, for like I said I see red and then
I am liable to do anything. I don't know my own
strength. Like the man at the approved school wrote
psychopath but I don't take much notice of that. But I
must know what it's all about, what we're here for, what
the Truth is. And sometimes I get so that I can't wait—
I *must* know. Often I've thought I've found it, but it's
been a bloody cheat. But I reckon I can learn a lot from
Huggett, because he's a genius. Well anyway that's
where I'm going now to the Italian coffee house to meet
The Crowd and not to bloody Southampton and home.
And Susan told Huggett it was my twenty-first birthday
and The Crowd is giving me a party. And mostly I don't
drink because I'm liable to get angry, but with The
Crowd I feel good and maybe I shall get drunk at my
party.

The Crowd sat at two long tables in the far corner of
the window. If the polished yet wilting rubber plant
which loomed above them had now the familiarity of the
aspidistra—once, after all, also a modish exotic—the un-
self-conscious dowdiness of the members of The Crowd
only seemed designed further to deny the tropical origin
of the fleshy leaves, to insist on their complete acclima-
tisation to the English lower-middle class world. Amid
the uniformity of elaborate male hair styles and female
horsehair tails, of jeans and fishermen's sweaters, the
dilapidated grammar school heartiness of The Crowds'
male attire, the dead but fussy genteelness of their women
might have suggested a sort of inverted exhibitionism.
But the clothes of The Crowd—the tired suits, the stained

B

flannels and grubby corduroys; the jumpers and skirts, the pathetically dim brooches and ear-rings—were no conscious protests, only the ends of inherited and accepted taste, the necessities of penurious earnings. Even Harold's blazer was just what he had always worn. They were as unconscious of the bejeaned world around them as they were of the rubber plant, the Chinese chequer players or the guitar of the skiffle group. They always met at the Italian coffee house and they drank Cona. They were as always talking; or rather the men were talking and the women were seeming to listen. Clothes were the last thing that either sex would have noticed in the other. The young women, except for Susan, were plain, and, except for Rosa, without make-up; but Rosa alone had a bad skin. The young men had strong faces with weak chins, except for Harold Gattley who was an older, simple-looking man with spectacles. He was probably over thirty. Huggett had a thin and freckled white face, unbrushed carroty hair, pale grey eyes and a rather feeble little reddish moustache. When, as now, the conversation had ceased to interest him, his face was quite without expression, his body absolutely still.

Reg was describing his present difficulties with his novel. "When Rawston gets back to London," he said, "he reads in the evening paper that there has been a big fire in Bristol, and a woman has been burned and he realises that it is Beth." He paused.

Everyone knew the plot and the characters of Reg's novel well, but Susan, who, had never shed an upper-middle class desire to say the right thing, asked, "Is that the whore?"

"Yes," said Reg. "What I'm worried about is Rawston's reaction. Beth had been the only living creature that he found when he returned home, the only being of force and will in Bristol, and by sleeping with her he'd renewed his energy. At the same time she represented the only claim the town and the past could make on him, now that his mother had married the school inspector and, of course, he had to destroy her. I don't know whether to make him remember that he'd overturned the oil stove before he left her lodging-house—a sort of subconscious half action that could be justifiable murder—or whether simply his will to be rid of her was enough to make her careless about the candle by her bed and so prepare her own destruction."

"If," observed Harold Gattley, "you give Rawston subconscious urges, you surely reduce his status as an expression of intellectually controlled will."

There was a general murmur of disapproval of the concept of the 'subconscious' and one man even suggested that it sounded dangerously like Freudian rubbish.

Huggett flicked into life for a moment, "I don't think Reg should be accused of infantilism," he said, "I imagine that by the subconscious he implies a reservoir of the Will that a man like Rawston, who is in training to realise himself, can call upon to strengthen his conscious powers. There are techniques for putting this reservoir more completely at command—prayer and contemplation and so on. I take it that Reg means Rawston to have some knowledge of these." There were disagreements between Huggett and Reg, but neither would have the other called a fool.

Reg nodded with a pleased smile, "Rawston," he said, "is not a homunculus, you know. He pitched old Daddy Freud with all the rest of the claptrap into the dung-heap long before the book begins. As Huggett says he knows the conventional exercises. Although, of course, he uses them for personal supremacy and not for all the old Christian rubbish. I have one chapter in which he reads Boehme and adapts his ideas for destructive ends."

Huggett closed his eyes wearily. "Oh God!" he cried, "all this dreary satanism, this nihilistic nonsense. You're just an old upside down romantic, Reg," and, when Reg was about to answer, "No, no. We can't argue about all that again now," Huggett said firmly, "What *does* worry me is all this conventional concern with individual per-sonalities. Rawston this and the harlot that. Of course, you've dug your own grave by using that rotting corpse, the novel. It's bound to be encumbered with humanistic dead wood."

"You need wood, Huggett, to make a fire," Reg answered in his special ruthless voice. "And, by God," he continued, "we'll light such a blaze that all their nice little civilised fire engines won't be able to put it out."

A frisson ran through the members of The Crowd present. The effect of Reg's and Huggett's talk on most of the girls and many of the men was always emotive rather than intellectual; it was always most powerful when the utterances were apocalyptic and mysteriously menacing to the old order.

Harold Gattley's new girl friend—a redhead—alone received no frisson; she was busily chasing with her tongue a seed that had lodged in her teeth. When she came to London to do a speech therapy course, she had determined to move in an artistic set, but this did not commit her to listening.

Susan, however, sought desperately for something nasty to say to Reg. She felt no sympathy with the ideas of The Crowd. She was held there solely by her strong physical desire for Reg and the hope that he would show interest in her again. Quiescence had proved no help and she had determined on a course of opposition to arouse him. She could think, however, of no comment except, "Take care you don't burn your fingers." It sounded a bit childish and, in any case, would only underline her schoolmarm manner which Reg and Huggett both despised. Eventually she said, "How boring all this intellectual pyromania is." But the words, which had seemed so sophisticated, came too late, for Reg had begun to talk again.

"Rawston," he said, "as soon as he reads the news, goes to the police and . . ." But the urges of Rawston's Heroic Will were to remain unrevealed, for at that moment Kennie entered the bar and made his way to their table.

Kennie's appearance, when as this evening he let his self-admiration have rein, caused comment even in the most extravagant worlds of jeans and hair does. Among The Crowd he seemed flagrant. His jeans were tighter than seemed altogether likely, and they were striped. His belt was bigger and more decked with brass studs. His sweater (the famous model) was unlikely ever to be repeated in its zebra-like weave. Beneath his swirling, sweeping mass of black hair, luxuriant with the strong scented 'Pour les hommes', his pale face was embarrassingly foolish and beautiful. His huge eyes stared vacantly, his wide sensual lips fell apart in a weak smile. Kennie always breathed through his mouth. He wore one small brass ear-ring. Above all, he was too short for so extravagant an attire. Reg frowned as Kennie took his seat by Susan and, as soon as the first greetings had finished, he continued, "You see, Rawston has to impose his will, at some point, on authority. . . ."

But Huggett would have none of it. He had adopted Kennie as idiot mascot and his mixed feelings of kindness and patronage were not going to have his pocket Myshkin pushed to one side by Reg. Huggett, he said to himself, was boss not Reg.

"Shut up, Reg," he said. "Damn your Rawston and all the other bloody little satanic nihilist heroes wreaking their puking little vengeances on Society. What better are they than a lot of damned Don Juans or Rastignacs or Sorels or the rest of the romantic rubbish? Keeping within the confines of their own clever little wills, their own bloody little sanities, their all too human clever tricks. Let them get the other side of sanity, that's where they'll find the Vision and the true Will, in Bedlam with old Billie Blake." And when Reg seemed about to reply, Huggett turned deliberately away from him, "Twenty-one-year-old Kennie," he said, "that's what we're celebrating to-day." It was final.

Susan took Kennie's hand. She had always aspired to teach the low I.Q.s, to reclaim the delinquents. Maternalism overwhelmed her and she hoped against hope that Reg's jealousy might be lit by taking it for more. She had even hoped once that the Maternalism would indeed

turn to something more, but Kennie had lain so passive
in their lovemaking, had rocked so cradle-content that
nothing had been woken in her. The Crowd had accepted
it as proof that Kennie was not queer and she had found
in it her first doubts. Nevertheless she squeezed his hand
and kissed him on the lips. "Many happy returns of the
day, darling," she said. And all the others, save Reg and
Rosa echoed her cry.

Kennie felt suddenly shy with The Crowd. He had
basked in their tolerance of him, feeling it as kindness that
had no strings attached—he believed that he had known
such things rarely in his life. But this sudden demonstra-
tion overwhelmed him. He wanted his party, of course,
but, above all, he wanted to hear The Crowd talk. He had
no liking for Reg, was indeed always glad to hear Huggett
wham him down; but Reg was still someone very important, the next to Huggett, and that his birthday should
be used to cut Reg's outpourings seemed to him almost
sacrilegious. Kennie had learned over many years to
please as well as to hate and he sought a way now to
please Reg. Nothing had surprised him more in his inter-
course with The Crowd than the numbers of plays and
novels and stories that the members were writing except
perhaps the strange names of their heroes—not Christian
names as in the books he had read but strange-sounding
surnames like Gorfitt, Sugden, Burlick and Rawston.
Knowing nothing of the D. H. Lawrence precedent, he
had worked out for himself that leaders, men with Will
perhaps, dispensed with Christian names—after all no one
ever spoke of anything but Huggett. Perhaps all these
strange characters in the books of The Crowd were a kind

of homage to Huggett. He had carefully memorised all their names. So now he turned to Reg and said with all the appeal he could muster, "I should imagine Rawston's a good deal like Sugden in Harold's play. I mean the way he does everything like for a purpose." Kennie's accent when he spoke was, unlike his grammar, very classy. Combined with his pretty looks it was all that Reg detested most.

"Oh, for God sake, Huggett," he cried, "if you want to believe all this Dostoevsky Myshkin balls, do you have to impose every little cretinous catamite on us? At least you can ask your protégé not to come the creeping jesus over me."

Susan and Huggett looked anxiously for a moment at Kennie; he had assured them so often of his 'seeing red' and of his ignorance of his own strength. Fortunately there were words he had not found in Havelock Ellis; he was clearly bewildered at Reg's outburst.

"Look, Reg," said Huggett authoritatively, " D. H. Lawrence was a fool. Happily for the world his corpse has long since mouldered. Don't bother to reincarnate it for us. You haven't got the right sort of beard." Then turning to Susan, he announced, "Vitelloni's for the celebration dinner, I think, don't you, Susan?" And in a few minutes The Crowd had swept Kennie off for an orgy of pasta, risotto and red chianti. It was all Reg could do to persuade Rosa to stay behind with him at the coffee house, as she said—"it's always silly to miss a party".

The idea, at first, was to go back to Huggett's room with plenty of bottles of Spanish red wine and play some records of unaccompanied Pennsylvania rail-road songs.

By the time, however, that they had reached the fruit salad and ice-cream, Huggett's elation produced another scheme. "Let's go to Clara's," he cried, "she'll lionise Kennie. You'd like to be lionised, wouldn't you?" A very little drink affected Huggett; his manner became almost bullying.

The delights of Vitelloni's food had soon palled on Kennie; he had no great taste for food and drink, but he was used to being given more luxurious meals than The Crowd knew. With a few glasses of wine, his mind had returned to his urgent quest for the Truth. "I wanted like to hear what *you* had to say," he told Huggett, and he confided to Susan, whose protective arm around his waist he was now beginning also to feel an encumbrance to his quest, "See I've not much time and I've got to find out such a lot about myself. I thought it might be that they'd be talking again about philosophy and truth and that."

"We shall," Huggett cried. "We shall talk of Truth and the true virtue of the Will until the small hours. But where better than at Clara's, Hetaira of Highgate, the Aspapia of the Archway. She holds the riddle of the Sphinx, Kennie, to say nothing of the secret of the Sibyls."

The Crowd goggled somewhat. One or two of the girls woke for a moment to hope and elation; Huggett seldom clowned, but when he did it meant only one thing —that he, who rigidly subordinated lust and, even more, emotion to the discipline of his great work, was in a sexy mood. The girls' hopes were soon dashed, however, for Huggett characteristically announced quite simply,

"Besides I think it's time that I took Clara to bed. She works too hard for the arts; she needs time off."

Huggett's laughter came rarely but when it did it was always sufficient for eight men. Normally, however, it was reinforced by laughter from all The Crowd; to-night there was no reinforcement. There was silence. Then one of the girls, forgetting Huggett's admonitions to Susan, said, "She's such an *awful* bourgeois creature, Huggett." Another said, "She must be quite old." They meant the same thing. A young man in a grubby leather jacket said, "It's slumming, Huggett, that's what it is." Harold Gattley blinked owlishly through his spectacles, "I expect she sleeps in silk sheets," he said, "just because she got your poems published, Huggett, there's no need to be that friendly." Clara Turnbull-Henderson in their view was both untouchable and out of range. Harold's red-haired girl finished manœuvring the last cherry in her fruit salad. She looked up and said primly, "I don't think I care to go all the way to Highgate, Harold."

Huggett was seldom faced with rebellion. On such occasions, he always seemed younger even than his twenty-two years. He ran his hand through his thick red hair in perplexity and stared at them in distress. Never-the-less he was determined, and he said with sudden, boyish heartiness, "She's got heaps of drink there— whisky, cherry brandy, crème de menthe." Then he got up from the table and edging through the narrow space between The Crowd and the next table, he made his way up the stairs, behind the cash desk to the dark, insani-tary lavatory that Vitelloni's provided for clients. Huggett's rare evasions were of the simplest kind.

Kennie, in whose life sex had been so frequent a burden, heard Huggett's proposal with disappointment and perplexity. He had felt so sure that to-night might be the crisis, the moment of revelation when he would learn what it was all about, what everything was for. And now perhaps there would be no talk. He thought of the unknown Clara with hatred. Susan's grey eyes rested on him maternally. She guessed his disappointment. She had almost decided to take Kennie off on her own, when Reg and Rosa silently took their places with The Crowd. Rosa's determination to be in on the party had won the day, but her fat little made-up face still wore the sulky pout by which she had gained her victory. Susan saw Reg and knew that she had to stay, but she pressed Kennie's knee, and said, "Don't worry. There'll be lots of talking, Kennie."

The Crowd pooled their money to pay for the meal, and, despite the prospect of Clara's drinks, bought bottles of red wine to take with them. They would not let Kennie pay for anything. They were eleven when they bundled into taxis for Highgate. Kennie had to pay at the other end, because The Crowd had now hardly five shillings between them. Paying for the taxis gave Kennie great pleasure, for he felt confident that he could come more easily by money than The Crowd could.

The Crowd surged up the front steps of Miss Turnbull-Henderson's large late-Regency stuccoed house. A small elderly man with flushed cheeks and greying black hair was already ringing the bell. He was soon swallowed up in the ocean of The Crowd's talk and, when the door opened, he was already being gradually levered backwards down the steps by the unheeding young people. The Italian maid—Miss Turnbull's fourth change in as many months—was completely incapable either of comprehending or of restraining The Crowd. When Clara herself arrived on the scene, The Crowd were already taking off the numerous scarves and gloves which both sexes wore at all times of the year. She was very disconcerted; her great dark eyes were round as a lemur's, her plump, young face blushed crimson with shyness and alarm, her long ear-rings shook. Her shyness became her; and even Kennie, struck with surprise at her prettiness, felt the soundness of Huggett's desires.

"We've brought some drink," said Huggett, "we're celebrating a twenty-first birthday. I remembered that after that meeting you told me you'd like to meet the rest of The Crowd."

"Oh, my dear," Clara cried and her silver dress shimmered and shook as she spoke, "I'm expecting Tristram Fleet." Then with more alarm, she cried, "Mr Fleet! Mr Fleet! There you are." She smiled with gracious, if excited welcome over the heads of The Crowd at the elderly stranger. Tristram Fleet smiled with equally gracious, old world courtesy back at her. In between was an insurmountable barrier of sports coats and duffle coats, woollen scarves and raincoats.

For a moment it seemed as though Mr Fleet and Clara were going to fight their way through to each other. But the situation was saved by Huggett. "I say," he said, "I had no idea you were Tristram Fleet. I'm Huggett and this is Reg Bellwood."

"How do you do?" said Mr Fleet. "May I say how

satisfying I found your poem 'St. John of the Cross', Mr
Huggett?"

"St John *on* the Cross," Reg said angrily, but Huggett
was genuinely delighted. "Thank you," he said, the
pleased little boy; then the angry small boy, he added,
"We're against most of the stuff you write, of course."

"Ah," Mr Fleet sighed, and he made a coy little moue.
"Ah well!"

It was beautifully done, Clara thought. Perhaps everything would be all right after all. To have brought
Huggett and his group into contact with Tristram Fleet
was quite something. What else was 'Mountside' for, for
what other purpose did all the money Mummy had left
her serve, except to create an intellectual forum? She had
been excited by the prospect of a tête-á-tête with Tristram
Fleet, but her excitement had been tinged with alarm.
Now she could simply assume the role of hostess to which
she had dedicated her life.

"Mr Huggett has already addressed the Club," she told
Tristram Fleet, and to Huggett she said, "Mr Fleet has
come to talk over a discussion I'm hoping to get up."
She left nothing for Huggett and Tristram Fleet to say.
But there was no fear of silence for The Crowd were
arguing loudly whether Fleet looked like his photographs,
whether it mattered whether he did or not, whether it
mattered *what* he looked like, whether, indeed, he mattered at all. Kennie was silent, for not reading either the
Sunday or the weekly book reviews he had never heard
of Tristram Fleet.

Harold's red-haired girl friend was silent, too; she
read all the Sunday and weekly book reviews and she

felt that at last she had *really* got into intellectual circles.

Only a few of her mother's Heal's chairs remained in the large drawing-room which Clara was converting to Brighton Pavilion chinoiserie. Mr Fleet, however, sat in one of the more comfortable of these, and devoted himself to a few words of compliment to his hostess about the dragon panels she had put in. "They're charmingly monstrous," he said, "but," he added, for in taste he made no demurs, "don't hesitate to let the whole thing be a hundred times more monstrous. I should like to see twisted dragons entwining everywhere in monstrous embraces. Especially on the ceiling."

This was no sort of talk for The Crowd and they set about consuming as much drink as they could in the shortest time. They persuaded Clara to let them make a 'cup' in a large china bowl. The Crowd always mixed as many types of drink together as possible—it saved precious time that might be spent in the fuss of choosing.

Tristram Fleet was nervous of The Crowd and in particular of Huggett. He would not otherwise have made his remark about the dragons and he quickly realised its unsuitability. He had accepted Miss Turnbull-Henderson's invitation to address her 'Readers and Writers Get Together Club' with some apprehension, but she offered such a good fee that he felt justified in considering it his duty. To find that one of the leaders of the new generation had already found the same duty cheered him, but he was not happy that his first meeting with Huggett should take place on such unfamiliar ground. At such times we would normally have taken refuge—a very congenial refuge—in making advances to one of the young women.

The girls of The Crowd, however, had naked faces and dirty hair; he was repelled by them. Clara's opulent, if rather goofy prettiness he found charming—he regretted their lost tête-á-tête. But to commit himself to Clara, with all the absurd implications of her celebrity hunting Club, before Huggett and The Crowd was a step he did not care to make. He was intensely relieved when Huggett squatted on the floor by his chair and began to make boyishly friendly conversation like any undergraduate fan. Soon they were discussing the economic possibilities in writing for a young man in modern England.

The Crowd relieved their nervousness of the chinoiserie by drinking continuously; Clara relieved her nervousness of The Crowd by filling their glasses as often as she could. A great deal was drunk very quickly.

Susan felt depressed because Reg and Rosa had begun smooching. She decided that it was abominable of Huggett so to neglect Kennie on his birthday treat. "This is Kennie Martin," she said to Clara, "it's *his* twenty-first birthday that we're celebrating."

If Clara found Kennie's clothes disconcerting, she thought his large-eyed face—a mixture of John Keats and cretinism—most disturbing. However she thought someone so 'interesting'-looking might well be a young genius. "I can't imagine anything more wonderful than to be twenty-one and have a whole creative future in front of you," she said.

Kennie did not answer. He was not, like The Crowd, particularly impressed by the chinoiserie, he had been been taken back to far grander places in his time—rooms with concealed cocktail cabinets and fitted-in bars.

Clara tried again. "Are you a dimanche writer?" she asked.

Kennie turned and stared at her. "See," he said, "I've got to listen to what Huggett's saying to that bloke. It's important to me."

Clara blushed crimson once more, but, remembering the strange brusqueries so usual in young genius, she decided not to take offence and contented herself by filling up Kennie's glass even more often than those of the others.

It was not long before Huggett's conversation changed from the polite and the practical to the expounding of doctrine. He had great faith in his powers of conversion. Tristram Fleet, lulled by preliminary politenesses, felt only flattered by this friendly man to man challenge of the avant garde. He was not among the established literary figures who made a profession of easy communication with youth; he only regretted now that more of his contemporaries were not present to witness his surprising success. He nodded attentively as Huggett gesticulated.

Kennie sat himself close to them and gazed as though into a fish tank at the Aquarium. Around this little group the smoke gathered and through it could be seen the increasingly drunk Crowd, petting and smooching, and occasionally sitting bolt upright to listen with drunken pantomimic reverence to the talk. Even Susan, with her short straggly hair and red sunburnt face, began to look like a tipsy cricket Blue. Through the haze Clara glided and glinted like some graceful, silvery fish. It was a success, she felt, but she did not dare to relax.

Kennie became increasingly sleepy. Huggett's dicta

came to him in sudden wafts and then receded. What he heard, however, semeed to his drunken senses the revelation he was seeking.

"There is no other vision but a subjective one," Huggett was saying, "I make my own maps and mark my own paths on them. If people choose to follow me they'll find their own salvation."

"But your secret areas are so closely guarded. You keep your secrets too well. You've published no Defence of the Realm Act," Mr Fleet said. It was all much easier than he had expected.

"It's my realm," Huggett shouted, and "I must protect it how I can."

Kennie saw how serious it all was from the look on Huggett's face. Later he heard Huggett protesting.

"Good God! Of course, Rousseau was insane. What would be the possible point of taking any notice of him, if he wasn't? If you sit on this side of sanity, you'll fade away with the anonymous men, you'll be lost in the desert void of reason. Surely you can see that the only hope lies in the subtle and difficult patterns that lie beyond the reason. Why even as an æsthete you must admit that. They're the only beautiful things left. Go to Blake, go to Maupassant in his last days, go to the Dukhobors and the followers of Jezreel. Why even the next lunatic escaped from an asylum can tell you more of what the real truth is than fools like Hume or Bertrand Russell."

"Mm," said Mr Fleet. "Great wits are sure to madness near allied. I see." It was all far more banal than he had expected. He was beginning to find it quite tedious.

C

Then again, through a thicker haze and a room that was increasingly showing signs of revolving Kennie heard Huggett say, "Oh well, of course, if you don't recognise the humanist conspiracy to conceal the truth they've betrayed."

"Do you seriously mean," Mr Fleet asked, "a conscious conspiracy?"

Huggett paused for a moment, then he replied gravely, "When I am talking to some people, I am inclined to think that the only answer to that question is, Yes."

"Ah," said Mr Fleet, "I see. Well that takes me into fields with which I'm quite unfamiliar and quite un-qualified to continue our argument." He got up and moved across the room.

Kennie could see that Huggett was very angry.

Distressed though he was at the course of his con-versation with Huggett, Tristram Fleet felt on his mettle not to give up. He came over to Reg. "And what are you writing at the moment, Mr Bellwood?" he asked.

Reg had been quite willing to be placated earlier, but he resented Tristram Fleet's sole attention to Huggett. He was annoyed with Rosa for making him come to the party and more deeply resentful than ever of Kennie as the cause of the occasion. He saw his chance. "Oh, nothing much. Thanks awfully," he said in an aggressive imitation of Mr Fleet's voice. Then taking Mr Fleet by the arm, he said, "But you must meet the hero of this party. Our twenty-one-year-old Teddy boy. I expect you've read about the menace of the Teddy boys, but I bet you've never met one, Mr Fleet."

He led the embarrassed critic over to where Kennie sat

with his sensual mouth more than usually adenoidally open in a desperate attempt to sort out Huggett's vital words from a general drink-fumed haze.

"Kennie," Reg said, "here's the most distinguished guest of your party—Mr Tristram Fleet. Mr Fleet, meet our twenty-one-year-old guest of honour, Kennie Martin, as you can see by his attire, a genuine guaranteed Teddy boy." He then moved away.

Kennie hated Reg for calling him a Teddy boy—everyone knew he was on his own. He remembered also that Tristram Fleet had made Huggett angry.

Mr Fleet's first impulse on taking in Kennie's appearance was to turn his back and go away, but the boy's evident misery made him feel that he must soften Reg Bellwood's rudeness. "I'm afraid that in my secluded ignorance," he said, "I've had no acquaintance with any of the young people of to-day—Teddy boys or otherwise. I'm delighted to meet you though. Many happy returns of the day."

Something in the combined cultured tones and evident nervousness of Mr Fleet gave Kennie a clue as to how he could avenge Huggett. He leaned forward in his chair and gave Mr Fleet a slow, insolent smile with which he had often sent elderly gentlemen about their business. "Look," he said, "you've got the wrong bloke. I shouldn't think you did know any Teddy boys, but if you did, I know what they'd call you—a f—— bent, see."

The slang was unfamiliar to Mr Fleet, but its intended meaning was painfully clear. He reddened with fury; his reputation was a womaniser was known to everyone. He turned his back on Kennie. For a moment he thought of leaving, but he somehow felt that he must restore his reputation. He looked for Clara, but to his disgust he saw that she had sunk at last on to the sofa where she was holding Huggett's hand. His eyes swept the hideous nakedness of the young women's faces. Harold's red-haired girl friend made a desperate effort to hold his glance, but he pushed on hurriedly. At last he fixed upon Rosa. Her face if a little spotty was, at least, properly made up and not without a certain sophistication. Her clothes too made some offer of the curves of her figure. Besides it would be pleasant to annoy the insufferable Mr Bellwood. He lowered himself with a certain difficulty to the floor by her chair, and gave her his full attention. Here he met with a greater triumph than perhaps he intended. Rosa was already disgruntled with her victory over Reg. So far it had given her no more than a little petting and, as this was from Reg himself, she might have had it less grudgingly anywhere else. Also she alone of the women of The Crowd felt any envy of Clara's looks, clothes and money. Attention from Tristram Fleet seemed at last to make sense of her triumph. She saw to it that at least she left in his taxi. Susan, too, gained indirectly from Rosa's triumph, for Reg could not bear to leave alone. Before Reg took her off, she bent over Kennie and asked, "Will you be all right, Kennie?" but he was asleep. Two by two The Crowd departed so that Huggett and Clara found themselves alone. When he began to unhook her dress she pointed at Kennie. Turning out the lights, she led Huggett upstairs.

It was quite dark in the room when Kennie woke. He felt very sick. His first thought was to get outside, for,

unless antagonised, he was naturally very polite and Clara
had been the hostess of The Crowd. It would be awful if
he vomited in her room, but he managed to hold off until
he got into the garden. Everything was very still when
he bent down under a lilac bush. When he raised his head
the sky seemed immense over him, the moonlight illu-
mined remote distances. Far away the sound of a train
whistle made his sense of loneliness almost unendurable.
He was near to tears. He fought through the daze to hold
on to the important things he had heard Huggett say. He
set off to walk across the Heath and work out their
meaning.

Colonel Lambourn looked at his watch and noted with
annoyance that it was already half-past midnight. He
liked to take his walk at half-past eleven exactly, but
recently he had fallen asleep once or twice after his dinner
and to-night he must have slept longer than usual. It was
not altogether surprising after the unsatisfactory chat he'd
had with that fellow at the Board of Trade—some subordinate without an ounce of gumption.

The Colonel locked the front door of his flat—always
rather a business now that he'd had a third lock put on,
but one couldn't be too careful with things as they stood
—and set off briskly along Parliament Hill to the Heath.
He carried his despatch-case with him, because despite
the three locks, there were things that he felt happier to
have under his eye—in fairness to the community. He
walked erectly and briskly for a man of seventy-four. He
was still a handsome man with his rubicund cheeks and
bright blue eyes, and he dressed smartly, although his

black hat and overcoat were not new. He noticed with satisfaction how quickly a sleep had restored his energies after a very tiring day. Visits to the central offices of the Prudential, to the Royal Geographical Society, to the Treasury, to the Board of Trade, to Peter Jones, to the Bolivian Embassy, to the Wallace Collection and to Church House—few men of his age could have carried programmes of this kind out day after day, wet or fine; but then few men of his age had his responsibilities, few men, indeed, of any age. He smiled grimly. His blue eyes had a watery glaze.

Reviewing the day's interviews—two events disturbed him; the incompetence of the subordinate at the Board of Trade, but, far more disturbing, the fellow at the Prudential. To begin with he had no illusions that the fellow was really the high-up chap he represented himself to be and he'd told him so, but more disturbing than that, he had a shrewd idea that it was the same fellow who'd represented himself to be the Curator of Kew Gardens a few days before, and indeed, the same chap that had given himself out to be the Secretary of the Patent Office last month. In which case . . . However, discipline was the main essential. Every step in the campaign in its due order; and no panic.

He went over to-morrow's appointments: Willesden Borough Council, the Lord Chamberlain's Office, the Directors of Overseas Broadcasts, the Scottish Office, the Ranger of Richmond Park, the Arts Council, Friends' House, and the Secretary of the Junior Carlton. A tiring day. The Colonel's eyelids shut, but a moment later he tensed the muscles of his face and marched on.

It was as he was passing a bench beneath a large oak tree that the Colonel's attention was drawn to a bent figure seated there. Some young fellow in distress apparently. Well, there'd soon be a great deal of distress in the world, unless the fellows in authority proved a great deal less idiotic than they had up to now. All the same, there was no more terrible sight in the world than a man in tears—most demoralising thing that could happen.

The Colonel was about to walk on, when some sense of his own distress and loneliness made him decide to see if he could help at all. Used as he was to official business, however, he was not adept at establishing human contacts. He sat rather stiffly at the other end of the bench and it was some minutes before he could bring himself to ask nervously, "Is there anything I can do to help?"

The boy turned enormous eyes upon him. "Look," he said, "I'm not interested."

Colonel Lambourn was familiar with these words. "I'm not surprised," he said, "few people are interested to find out the truth." To his amazement however, the boy took him up on these words.

"Who says I'm not interested in the Truth. That's what I'm searching for, see."

"Ah!" said Colonel Lambourn. "In that case . . ." He felt in his breast pocket, took out a leather wallet and presented the boy with his card. "Lieutenant-Colonel Lambourn (Rtd), 673, Parliament Hill, N.W."

The boy read the card then he said, "I thought you looked like a colonel." But Colonel Lambourn no longer seemed interested in the boy's remarks, he opened his despatch-case and began to take out various maps. He spoke in a loud, rather colourless, official voice, "I'm perfectly aware, sir," he said, "that you are a very busy man." The boy looked surprised at this, "As I am myself," the Colonel went on, "I shall not presume any further on your time than it takes to explain the essentials of the very serious situation which at present presents itself in this country. A situation which, however, I think you will see offers unlimited possibilities if comprehended properly and dealt with promptly. A situation which if, as I say, dealt with in this way offers to humanity a greater opportunity of grasping the essential truth of life than any that have previously existed. And now," he said and his watery blue eyes glinted with a formal smile, "I shall cut out any further cackle and draw your attention to these three maps."

He seemed for a moment to search for a table in front of him, then contenting himself with the ground, he spread out a map of England. "I do not have to remind you, sir," he said, "of the absolute secrecy which necessarily surrounds my statement. I don't wish," he looked a little anxiously at the boy and his head shook a little, "to speak idly of a conspiracy. People are so often discouraged when I tell them of the continuous persecution to which I've been subjected." His voice sounded puzzled, "Fools find it so easy to avoid the truth by calling it madness."

The boy looked at the old man eagerly, then he asked with excitement, "Have you ever been in an asylum?"

Colonel Lambourn drew himself up stiffly, "My enemies," he said, "had me locked away at one time, but

I'm glad to say justice prevailed." He folded up the map and showed signs of leaving.

"No, don't go," the boy cried, "I want to hear what you have to say. Like you'll be able to tell the truth of it all."

The old man spread out the map once more. "Thank you for your understanding, sir," he said, "you are a wise man." And now he began to explain the red lines and crosses on the map. "These you see," he said, "are the old bridle paths of the eighteenth and nineteenth centuries. As far as I have been able to establish them," and he repeated somewhat vaguely, "As far as I have been able to establish them. Now," and he spread out another map marked in blue, "here you have the Government defence zones, atomic power stations and gun sites laid down in the Defence of the Realm Act."

The boy's eyes grew rounder as Huggett's conversation with Fleet returned to him.

"You will notice that each of these bridle paths leads in fact to a defence zone. Hardly a coincidence, I suggest. Now look at this third map. A Map of Treasure Trove issued by the Office of Works. Notice the position of the bridle paths in relation to the buried treasures and in relation to the defence zones." The boy echoed, "Buried treasure," excitedly, "But," said the old man solemnly, "this map perhaps is the most conclusive. A diagram of the intersections of the three maps when superimposed. You see what they show?" he asked.

The boy stared open-mouthed.

"No?" said the Colonel. "Allow me to draw your attention. So, so, and so. You see. Three open pentacles."

He sat back with a look of triumph. And the boy leaned forward excitedly.

"I think," Colonel Lambourn said, "that if the intersections of these pentacles themselves were to be fully explored, indeed I have no doubt, that humanity would be in possession of what I may call the putative treasure and, if that were to happen, I have no doubt that our enemies would be, to put it mildly, seriously discomforted." He began to fold up the maps and replace them in the despatch-case.

"What's it mean?" cried the boy. "What's it tell you?" And as the old man began to rise from the bench, he seized his arm roughly, "I want to know the Truth," he cried, "I want you to tell me the Truth of it all. What's behind it?"

Colonel Lambourn turned and stared at the boy. His head shook a little and for a moment a film came down over his blue eyes, then he sat down, opened his despatch-case and took out the first map. The boy's body trembled with excitement. "I'm perfectly aware, sir," the Colonel said, "that you are a very busy man. As I am myself. So I shall not presume any further on your time than it takes to explain the essentials of the very serious situation which at present presents itself in this country. . . ." The boy stared amazed. "A situation which, however," the Colonel went on, "I think you will see offers possibilities."

"It's a bloody cheat," Kennie cried.

The despair of his screams made the Colonel turn towards him. Kennie banged his fist down on the old man's face. Blood poured from the Colonel's nose and

he fell backwards, hitting his head on the bench corner.
Kennie got up and ran away across the grass.

See, it's like I said when I see red I don't know my own
strength. And it's all, all of it, a bloody cheat and I don't
know what I shall do. But if there's questions, I'll be all
right, see, because what's an old bloke like that want
talking to me on Hampstead Heath at one o'clock in the
morning. That's what they'll want to know.

A Flat Country Christmas

As usual Carola had to run back into the bungalow two or three times before they were ready to set off. First, she had forgotten her hanky, and then she thought she had put the hot plate on at 'medium' instead of 'low' for Mrs Ramsden's stew, lastly she was sure she had told the old lady wrong about the time for Deirdre's bottle. As a rule Ray used these delays to memorise for his exam, running over one of the set schemes for the General Paper that the Correspondence School had sent him, or reconstructing a chapter from the Hammonds—he expected to do rather well on the Industrial Revolution. Sometimes, when his headaches were bad, he tapped on the gate-post or called after Carola in the sharp, peremptory voice he had acquired as an officer. But this afternoon, although his head was splitting, his whole body seemed to resist any contact with the outside world. He merely stood, sucking at his empty pipe, and staring at the houses around him.

Even on this unnaturally bright and sunny Christmas night of 1949, the rows of bungalows and council houses seemed silently disapproving, forbiddingly reserved. The Slaters' home stood on the very edge of the estate, com-

manding a panorama of flat, marshy fields, broken here
and there by a muddy stream or a huge oak in the last
decay of majesty—merging at last into the faint shining
vermilion of the roofs of the next 'new town' some three
miles away.

Carola's first reaction, as she saw the depression of
Ray's stance, was to slip her arm through his and call his
attention to 'their view'. With her new French blue
costume and red leather belt she felt very certain of
herself; even her lipstick, she thought, was right for
once, would give no hint of the Chapel background
of which she was always too aware when they visited
Sheila.

In so unusual a mood of self-assurance, she was more
than ever proud of the position of the bungalow, so
almost in the country. But as she looked again at the
shapeless waste land before her, some faint breath of
melancholy and despair seeped even into her busy
chattering world; she blew it aside with a gust of solicitude for her husband. "You haven't got a temperature,
have you, darling?" she asked, and put her cool little
hand up to his brow. Ray only removed his pipe and
said, "No." There was nothing Carola feared more than
being a fusspot—not understanding, or nagging like the
old Chapel cats; so she decided just to chatter on—Ray's
funny little mouse. She was glad they were going to
Eric and Sheila because they were such old friends, only
she did hope there wouldn't be any politics. . . .

It was really just the neighbourhood to start life in, she
thought, as they made their way across the marshes. They
didn't know anybody, of course, even after a year's

residence, but at least there was none of the prying and
gossip of her village home. Yes, an ideal place to start life
in, so long as you didn't get stuck. But there wasn't much
likelihood of that, she decided, as she looked at Ray's tall,
upright figure, his clear-cut features and steady reliable
blue eyes—a Technical Officer at the Ministry and about
to take an Honours degree.

As if to echo her thoughts, Ray's voice cut across her
chatter about Deirdre's attempts at speech. "I've applied
for the Inspectorship," he said in his usual clear, confident voice, but a shade more loudly to cover his
depression with words.

"With the degree behind me, I shall still be able to sit
the Administrative in June. But it'll be the last Reconstruction entrance, and it's just as well to have a second
string. Don't say anything to Eric. He's got some bee in
his bonnet about sticking in the Technical Grade until
the Association's taken the new claim to arbitration. He
talks about it as a moral issue, as if *that* had any meaning.
He's so unrealistic. We'll get from the Treasury exactly
what they can give us, which at the moment is what
we're already getting. I hope to God he doesn't start on
it to-night. Rights to this and Rights to that: he's still
with Tom Paine. He and the old man ought to get together. Did you see Dad's last letter? He's back to Keir
Hardie now, and how we aren't a 'fighting party' any
more. He'd do better fighting for Mother to have a bit
of a rest."

Carola tucked her arm into his. "I know, darling," she
said, and somewhere from her Baptist girlhood her
mother's voice reached her. Pursing up her lips defiantly

she added, "As if we aren't all Labour, but we don't have to shout about it."

They had left the fields now and were passing through the overgrown shrubbery of some demolished nineteenth-century mansion. Through the rhododendrons and the laurels they could see the by-pass, its white concrete line of shops shining in the dying light—the snack bar, the Barclay's bank, the utility furniture store, Madame Yvonne's beauty parlour.

At last they turned into the drive of a small Edwardian house. The lawn was planted with standard roses, but the conservatory stood glassless and derelict. The half-timbered upper storey of the house was a bold black and white, in the porch hung a wrought iron lantern. Ray stopped dead in the middle of his loud discourse on his future, his thin lips and heroic eyes resumed their set of misery, then as suddenly grimaced into manly matiness. "I could use a drink just about now," he said, and, giggling, Carola answered, "I hope Sheila doesn't make them as strong as last time."

Sheila, of course, had. If you have drinks have them good, was only one of the many solid maxims of her rich Guildford business background that she had tried so hard but had failed to shed. She embodied three generations of business success—her own plain black dress and gay Jacqmar scarf speaking for bookish Roedean and Girton, something in her over-cultured voice for her mother's feverish W.V.S. attempts to "make the county", and deep down a vulgar rumble that declared her grandmother's over-jewelled, nouveau riche toughness.

"How are you, darling?" She kissed Carola, "and little Deirdre?"

"Terribly naughty, I'm afraid," said Carola, meaning really that as usual she was afraid of Sheila.

"That comes of feeding her on meat." Eric's cockney voice was at the top of his Max Miller form, his absurdly young face wore its most cheeky errand boy look. He did not want a row with Ray, yet the news weighed on him so heavily that he doubted if he could avoid it. Only clowning, perhaps, could help; he would give them his every imitation from 'Eton and Oxford' to the flushing of the lavatory cistern, and so, perhaps, carry the evening through.

And now the party got under way. It was a curiously formal measure for close friends—rigid in its pattern like some saraband or pavane. They had broken down so many social barriers and prejudices to get there, and in the strange, flat isolation of the housing estate they depended so much on these bonds forged in the now distant days in the Forces. They felt justly proud of the emancipation from class that they had achieved both in marriage and in friendship, but, though they had no wish to live on sentiment and memory, these were the only cement that riveted the fortress they had constructed against loneliness.

First, then, it must be ladies to the centre. Carola would admire the simplicity of Sheila's table-setting, though she wondered strangely at the lack of doilies, of little mats and of colourfully arranged salads and fruit that she copied so carefully from women's magazines. Sheila must praise Carola's new blue dress, and wish that she could speak about the dreadful little doggy brooch. She would first blame herself for snobbery, and then decide that after all there was nothing morally right about bad taste and petty bourgeois gentility. They were happier when they got on to Ray's headaches, about which they could both be sensible, psychological and practical. "What did the clinic say?" and, "Oh, but that's the whole point. You can get decent psychiatric treatment now without being a millionaire." It was nice, they both thought, when common ground could be reached, because they did like each other, only they were rather thrown together.

Gentlemen to the side, meanwhile, were carefully avoiding politics. It was chaff and office personalities, and when these threatened to get too warm, questions from Eric about Robert Owen, and Ray trying to please by saying "but the only really good analysis of course was Engel's 1844". They could compromise and please one another as long as they stuck to the nineteenth century, giving full rein to the mutual admiration they had acquired in the army.

And now it was lady to gentleman. Sheila and Ray talked books. She, perhaps, found his approach a bit utilitarian. "I know," she said, "about comparing Fielding and Richardson, and Dickens and Thackeray, but I still don't think it's very helpful." After all, he decided, it was easy enough for her to say "damn Leavis, she still didn't think Conrad was any good"; she hadn't got to take the Reconstruction English paper. On the whole, however, they kept in step very well and were proud of their part of the measure. For Carola and Eric it was not easy. He thought her a nice little thing, but as heavy as a

D

suet pudding and far too like one in the face. She wished so much she didn't think him common. But they managed all right on praise of Ray and Sheila, and glowed at each other in the process.

Finally it was all together to the centre with stories of the old War days and a good time had by all.

It wasn't Christmas every day, so they toasted "Absent Friends". Each now slid away in a pas seul of memory, back to the stifling family Christmas ritual from which they had escaped.

"Absent friends," Carola's mother had said as she raised her glass of ginger wine, "and I'm sorry so many of them should have been absent from Chapel this morning."

"If you mean Penelope," Carola had replied red in the face above her gym tunic, "she was skating. After all the river isn't frozen every Christmas; is it so very serious for once?"

"It's pennies that make pounds, my dear. You can give a little here and a little there, and in the end there's nothing in the bank."

"Absent friends," Sheila's grandmother had said with a snort, "I suppose Sheila's thinking of her Mugginses or Fugginses or whatever they're called. A nice rumteyfoo lot, not a penny to bless themselves with."

"Hush, darling," said Sheila's mother; "we don't use expressions like that now. All the same, Sheila, I do think they're rather a tatty crowd."

"I don't understand what you mean," said Sheila obstinately.

"I think you do, darling," replied her mother. "There

are standards—gracious living, you know—that are surely worth something. It seems terrible to throw it all away unless you're very sure you've got something to put in its place."

"Absent friends!" Ray's father had said. "To the boys of the International Brigade, and damnation to Non-Intervention." Ray felt his collar stick to his neck. Of course, he was against Franco, but what a moment to choose, and the sentimentality of it.

"Absent friends," Eric's spiv brother had said, "and from what I've seen of Eric's mob, the longer the bleeders are absent, the better."

Well, now it was these families who were absent; the friends had been kept through all the hazards of class. They felt warmer to each other, after their lonely childhood dances were over. There might be faults here and there, but their friendship was built on a common way of living—tolerant, forward-looking, never anti-social. Eric turned on the wireless to dispel the last clouds of melancholy. "Enjoy yourself, enjoy yourself, it's later than you think," sang the vocalist. It was then that Ray first lost control. Turning off the wireless abruptly, "I'm sorry I don't think I can stand that," he said. The others searched about for a means of passing over the incident, and they fell back almost automatically upon a familiar dirge.

Carola spoke first; she felt she must excuse Ray's behaviour. "I don't think the air down here does Ray any good," she said.

"It's awfully depressing," Sheila agreed, "I think that's why there's so little going on in the place."

"Yes," said Carola, "you'd think there'd be a dramatic society or something," and she took Ray's hand, for they had met in a Forces show.

"Everyone seems half asleep," said Sheila.

"Asleep," said Eric, "they call a man a live wire if he's only been dead three weeks."

They waited for Ray to speak, it was his buoyancy and confidence that usually carried them out of this mood. But his voice, when it came, was from the tomb, "It's such very flat country," he said.

Carola, once again, felt impelled to lead the party up to the heights. "Oh, well," she said brightly, "we're not likely to stick here long."

"God, no," said Sheila, "Eric's only waiting for the arbitration decision to apply for a move."

"That's right," said Eric, "and another thing, the Ministry won't be able to stand out long against the return to London. Devolution's had it . . ." But he stopped in the middle of the sentence. Illogically perhaps, he found that the name of London always brought the atom bomb to his mind. He'd been wanting to speak of it all the evening, but he'd promised Sheila to keep off it. They waited more than ever on Ray now, but he just stared into the distance.

"I've thought of the silliest thing," said Carola. She had to say something to cover Ray's silence. "Could we take one of the mirrors down, Sheila?"

"Of course, darling, but whatever for?"

"Well, I read about it in *Woman's Own* or somewhere. You decorate a mirror with mistletoe on Christmas Night and it acts as a sort of crystal to gaze in."

"Oh, do let's try," cried Sheila. Any port in a storm, she thought.

Even Eric seemed enthusiastic. "What the Stars Foretell. Why not? I'm all for it."

But when Sheila looked into the mirror, she could make nothing of it. "I'm afraid it's no good, darling," she said, "I never was psychic. Except that I do see how like Queen Elizabeth I am. My nose is fantastic."

Carola in her turn wasn't sure, but she really thought the mirror did get a bit cloudy, and she saw something awfully like a baby.

"Hundred of darling little Deirdres, I expect," said Sheila rather sharply.

"Hallelujah," cried Eric as he bent over the glass, "fourteen Lana Turners doing the Veil Dance. And a kick in the pants for MacArthur, Deakin and Ernie B. This is Heaven all right. Open up dem pearly gates, I'se a coming, Lord."

They were all quite surprised when Ray agreed to sit down before the mirror, but he sat so long and so silently, that they decided to disregard him.

"Well, I'll go and get me the wallop," said Eric. The sooner the evening was ended the better.

It was only the sound of Ray's sobbing that finally woke them to his condition.

"Ray!" cried Carol. "What's wrong, my darling?"

Ray's gaze was blank when he turned to them; only the tears running down his cheeks seemed alive. "Oh! My God!" he said. "Oh! My God! I've seen Nothing!"

"My poor poppet," said Sheila, all understanding. "Never mind. Come and sit down." But Ray just continued to cry. "Darling, you must get him home," said Sheila.

Carola was so miserable and embarrassed. "If you won't think it awful. . . ."

"My dear," said Sheila, practical, never alarmist, "there's nothing to worry about. He's just overworked. But you must put him to bed and get Doctor Rayesley. I'll ring Quiktax now."

Eric couldn't help it, he'd suppressed his apolalyptical thoughts so long, and now he said, "I know what. Ray's seen the future and we've all been atomised." It was a facetiousness he would never forgive himself. But Ray only shook his head.

"That's all to do with you. I'm not concerned with it. This is personal. I've felt it somewhere about for weeks. perhaps years, and now I've seen it. I've seen Nothing."

Carola's embarrassment was more than she could bear. "You old silly," she said, "we none of us saw anything. Sheila *said* so, and Eric was only joking. And as for me you know I can imagine anything."

Ray turned on her savagely, "Why are you talking?" he shouted. "It doesn't matter to me what you do or say." He broke off as suddenly, "I'm sorry," he said. "It's not of any importance," and he stared into the fire.

More Friend than Lodger

AS soon as Henry spoke of their new author Rodney Galt I knew that I should dislike him. "It's rather a feather in my cap to have got him for our list," he said. The publishing firm of which Henry is a junior partner is called Brodrick Layland which as a name is surely a feather in no one's cap, but that by the way. "I think Harkness were crazy to let him go," Henry said, "because although *Cuckoo* wasn't a great money-spinner, it was very well thought of indeed. But that's typical of Harkness, they think of nothing but sales."

I may say for those who don't know him that this speech was very typical of Henry: because, first, I should imagine most publishers think a lot about sales and, if Brodrick Layland don't, then I'm sorry to hear it; and, secondly, Henry would never naturally use expressions like "a great money spinner", but since he's gone into publishing he thinks ought to sound a bit like a business man and doesn't really know how. The kind of thing that comes natural to Henry to say is that somebody or something is "very well thought of indeed", which doesn't sound like a business man to anyone, I imagine. But what Henry is like ought to emerge from my story if I'm able to write it at all. And I must in fairness add that

49

my comments about him probably tell quite a lot about me—for example he isn't by any means mostly interested in the money in publishing but much more in "building up a good list", so that his comment on Harkness wasn't hypocritical. And, as his wife, I know this perfectly well, but I've got into the habit of talking like that about him.

Henry went on to tell me about *Cuckoo*. It was not either a novel, which one might have thought, or a book about birds or lunatics, which was less likely, although it's the kind of thing I might have pretended to think in order to annoy him. No, *Cuckoo* was an anthology and a history of famous cuckolds. Rodney Galt, it seemed, had a great reputation, not as a cuckold, for he was single, but as a seducer; although his victories were not only or even mainly among married women. He was particularly successful as a matter of fact at seducing younger daughters and debs. Henry told me all this in a special offhand sort of voice intended to suggest to me that at Brodrick Layland's they took that sort of thing for granted. Once again I'm being bitchy, because, of course, if I had said "Come off it, Henry" or words to that effect, he would have changed his tone immediately. But I did not see why I should, because among our acquaintances we *do* number a few though not many seducers of virgins; and if I made Henry change his tone it would suggest that he was *quite* unfamiliar with such a phenomenon which would be equally false. Fairness and truth are my greatest difficulties in life.

To return to Rodney Galt—the book he was going to write for Brodrick Layland was to be called *Honour and Civility*. Once again it was not to be a novel, however, like *Sense and Sensibility* or *The Naked and the Dead*. Rodney Galt used the words 'honour' and 'Civility' in a special sense; some would say an archaic sense, but he did not see it that way because he preferred not to recognise the changes that had taken place in the English language in the last hundred years or so. 'Honour' for him meant 'the thing that is most precious to a man', but not in the sense that the Victorians meant that it was most precious to a woman. Rodney Galt from what I could gather would have liked to see men still killing each other in duels for their honour and offering civilities to one another in the shape of snuff and suchlike before they did so. He believed in 'living dangerously' and in what is called 'high courage', but exemplified preferably in sports and combats of long standing. He was, therefore, against motor racing and even more against 'track' but in favour of bull-fighting and perhaps pelota; he was also against dog racing but in favour of baccarat for high stakes.

The book, however, was not to be just one of those books that used to be popular with my uncle Charles called *Twelve Rakes* or *Twenty Famous Dandies*. It was to be more philosophical than that, involving all the author's view of society; for example, that we could not be civilised or great again unless we accepted cruelty as a part of living dangerously, and that without prejudice man could have no opinion, and, indeed, altogether what in Mr Galt's view constituted the patrician life.

I told Henry that I did not care for the sound of him. Henry only smiled, however, and said, "I warn you that he's a snob, but on such a colossal scale and with such panache that one can't take exception to it." I told Henry firmly that I was not the kind of woman who could see things on such a large scale as that, and also, that if, as I suspected from his saying "I warn you", he intended to invite Rodney Galt to the house, only the strictest business necessity would reconcile me to it.

"There *is* the strictest business necessity," Henry said, and added, "Don't be put off by his matinee idol looks. He's indecently good-looking." He giggled when he said this, for he knew that he had turned the tables on me. Henry used to believe—his mother taught him the idea— that no woman liked men to be extremely good-looking. He knows different now because I have told him again and again that I would not have married him if he had not been very handsome himself. His mother's code, how- ever, dies hard with him and even now, I suspect, he thinks that if his nose had not been broken at school, I should have found him too perfect. He is quite wrong. I would willingly pay for him to have it straightened if I thought he would accept the offer.

Reading over what I have written, I see that it must appear as though Henry and I live on very whimsical terms—gilding the pill of our daily disagreements with a lot of private jokes and 'sparring' and generally rather ghastly arch behaviour. Thinking over our life together, perhaps it is true. It is with no conscious intent, however; although I have read again and again in the women's papers to which I'm addicted that a sense of humour is the cement of marriage. Henry and I have a reasonable proportion of sense of humour, but no more. He gets his, which is dry, from his mother who, as you will see in this story of Rodney Galt, is like a character from the novels of Miss Compton Burnett, or, at least, when I read those novels I people them entirely with characters like Henry's mother. My parents had no vestige of humour; my father was too busy getting rich and my mother was too busy unsuccessfully trying to crash county society.

But it *is* true that Henry and I in our five years of marriage have built up a lot of private joking and whimsical talking and I can offer what seem to be some good reasons for it, but who am I to say? First, there is what anyone would pick on—that our marriage is childless, which, I think, is really the least of the possible reason. It certainly is with me, although it may count with Henry more than he can say. The second is that everything counts with Henry more than he can say. 'Discerning' people who know Henry and his mother and, indeed, all the Ravens, usually say that they are shy beneath their sharp manner. I don't quite believe this; I think it's just because they find it easier to be like this so that other people can't overstep the mark of intimacy and intrude too far on their personal lives. You can tell from the way Henry's mother shuts her eyes when she meets people that she has an interior life and actually she is a devout Anglican. And Henry has an interior life which he has somehow or other put into his publishing. Well, anyhow, Henry's manner shy or not makes me shy, and I've got much more whimsical since I knew him.

But also there's my own attitude to our marriage. I can only sum it up by saying that it's like the attitude of almost everyone in England to-day to almost everything. I worked desperately hard to get out of the insecurity of my family—which in this case was not economic because they're fairly rich and left me quite a little money of my own, but social—and when I married Henry I loved every minute of it because the Ravens are quite secure in their own way—which Henry's mother calls "good country middle class, June dear, and no more". And if that security is threatened for a moment I rush back to it for safety. But most of the time when it's not in danger, I keep longing for more adventure in life and a wider scope and more variety and even greater risks and perils. Well, all that you'll see in this story, I think. But anyhow this feeling about our marriage makes me uneasy with Henry and I keep him at a humorous distance. And he, knowing it, does so all the more too. All this, I hope, will explain our private jokes and so on, of which you will meet many. By the way, about security and risk, I don't really believe that one can't have one's cake and eat it—which also you'll see.

To return to Rodney Galt; Henry did, in fact, invite him to dinner a week later. He was not, of course, as bad as Henry made out, that is to say, as I have sketched above, because that description was part of Henry's ironical teasing of me. In fact, however, he was pretty bad. He said ghastly things in an Olympian way—not with humour like Henry and me, but with 'wit' which is always rather awful. However, I must admit that even at that first dinner I didn't mind Rodney's wit as much as all that, partly because he had the most lovely speaking voice (I don't know why one says speaking voice as though most of one's friends used recitative) very deep and resonant which always 'sends' me; and partly because he introduced his ghastly views in a way that made them seem better than they were. For example:

Henry said, "I imagine that a good number of your best friends are Jews, Galt."

And Rodney raised his eyebrows and said, "Good heavens, why?"

And Henry answered, "Most anti-Semitic people make that claim."

And Rodney said, "I suppose that's why I'm not anti-Semitic. I can't imagine knowing any Jews. When would it arise? Oh, I suppose when one's buying pictures or objects, but then that's hardly knowing. It's simply one of the necessities. Or, of course, if one went to Palestine, but then that's hardly a necessity."

And I said, "What about Disraeli? He made the Tory party of to-day." I said this with a side glance at Henry because he used then to describe himself as a Tory Democrat, although since Suez he has said that he had not realised how deeply Liberalism ran in his veins.

Rodney said, "What makes you speak of such unpleasant things?"

And I asked, "Aren't you a Tory then?"

And he answered, "I support the principles of Lord Eldon and respect the courage of Lord Sidmouth, if that's what you mean."

Henry said, "Oh! but what about the Suez Canal and the British Empire? Disraeli made those."

And Rodney looked distant and remarked, "The British Empire even at its height was never more than a convenient outlet for the middle-class high-mindedness of Winchester and Rugby. The plantations and the penal colonies of course," he added, "were a different matter."

Henry, who makes more of his Charterhouse education than he admits, said, "Oh, come, Winchester and Rugby are hardly the same thing."

Rodney smiled and said in a special hearty voice, "No, I suppose not, old man." This was rude to Henry, of course, but slightly gratifying to me. Anyhow he went straight on and said, "The thing that pleases me most about coming to Brodrick Layland is your book production, Raven, I do like to feel that what I have written, if it is worth publishing at all, deserves a comely presentation." This, of course, was very gratifying to Henry. They talked about books or rather the appearance of books for some time and I made little comment as I like the inside of books almost exclusively. It appeared, however, that Rodney was a great collector of books, as he was of so many other things: porcelain, enamels, Byzantine ivories and Central American carvings. He was quick to tell us, that, of course, with his modest income he had to leave the big things alone and that, again with his modest income, it was increasingly difficult to pick up anything worth having, but that it could be done. He left us somehow with the impression that he would not really have cared for the big things anyway, and that his income could not be as modest as all that.

"Heaven defend me," he said, "from having the money to buy those tedious delights of the pedants—incunables. No, the little Elzeviers are my particular favourites, the decent classical authors charmingly produced. I have a delightful little Tully and the only erotica worth possessing, Ovid's *Amores*."

It was talking of Ovid that he said something which gave me a clue to my feelings about him.

"I know of no more moving thing in literature than Ovid's exiled lament for Rome. It's just how any civilised Englishman to-day must feel when, chained to his native land, he thinks of the Mediterranean or almost anywhere else outside England for that matter. 'Breathes there a Soul,' you know." He smiled as he said it. Of course, it was the most awful pretentious way of talking, but so often I do feel that I would rather be almost anywhere than in England that he made me feel guilty for not being as honest as he was.

It seemed, however, that after a great deal of travel in a great many places, he *was* now for some time to be chained to his native land. He had, he said, a lot of family business to do. He was looking out for a house something like ours. He even hinted—it was the only hint of his commercially venturing side that he gave that evening —at the possibility of his buying a number of houses as an investment. Meanwhile he was staying with Lady Ann Denton. I ventured to suggest that this might be a little too much of a good thing, but he smiled and said that she was a very old friend, which, although it rather put me in my place, gave him a good mark for loyalty. (Henry scolded me afterwards and told me that Rodney was having an affair with Lady Ann. This surprised and disconcerted me. It didn't sound at all like 'debs'. Lady Ann is old—over forty—and very knocked about and ginny. She has an amusing malicious tongue and a heart of gold. Sometimes I accept her tongue because of her heart, and sometimes I put up with her heart because of her tongue. Sometimes I can't stand either. But, as you will have already seen, my attitude to people is rather ambiguous. However, Henry is very fond of her. She makes him feel broadminded which he likes very much.)

We had it out a little about snobbery that evening. "Heavens, I should hope so," Rodney said, when I accused him of being a social snob, "it's one of the few furies worth having that are left to us—little opportunity though the modern world allows of finding anyone worth cultivating. There still do exist a few families, however, even in this country. It lends shape to my life as it did to Proust's." I said that though it had lent shape to Proust's work, I wasn't so sure about his life. "In any case," he said with a purposeful parody of a self-satisfied smile, "art and life are one." Then he burst out laughing and said, "Really, I've excelled myself this evening. It's your excellent food."

Looking back at what I have written I see that I said that he wasn't as bad as Henry made out and then everything that I have reported him as saying is quite pretentious and awful. The truth is that it was his smile and his good looks that made it seem all right. Henry had said that he was like a matinee idol, but this is a ridiculous expression for nowadays (whatever it may have been in the days of Henry's mother and Owen Nares) because no one could go to a matinee with all those grey-haired old ladies up from the Country rattling tea-trays and feel sexy about anything. But Rodney was like all the best film stars rolled into one and yet the kind of person it wasn't surprising to meet; and, these taken together surely make a very sexy combination.

It was clear that evening that Henry liked him very much too. Not for that reason, of course, Henry hasn't ever even thought about having feelings of that kind I'm glad to say. As a matter of fact, Henry doesn't have sexy feelings much anyway. No, that's quite unfair and bitchy of me again. Of course, he has sexy feelings, but he has them at definite times and the rest of the time such things don't come into his head. Whereas I don't ever have such strong sexy feelings as he has, but I have some of them all the time. This is a contrast that tends to make things difficult.

No, the reason Henry liked him I could see at once, and I said as soon as he had left, "Well, he's quite your cup of tea, isn't he? He's been everywhere and knows a lot about everything." I said the last sentence in inverted commas, because it's one of Henry's favourite expressions of admiration and I often tease him about it. It isn't very surprising because Henry went to Charterhouse and then in the last two years of the War he went with the F.S.P. to Italy, and then he went to the Queen's College, Oxford, and then he went into Brodrick Layland. So he hasn't been everywhere. In fact, however, he does know quite a lot about quite a number of things, but as soon as he knows something he doesn't think it can be very important.

We both agreed then that Rodney Galt was quite awful in most ways but that we rather liked him all the same. This is my usual experience with a great number of people that I meet, but Henry found it more surprising.

In the weeks that followed Henry seemed to see a good deal of Rodney Galt. He put him up for his Club. I was

E

rather surprised that Rodney should have wanted to be a member of Henry's Club which is rather dull and literary: I had imagined him belonging to a lot of clubs of a much grander kind already. Henry explained that he did in fact belong to a lot of others, but that he had been abroad so much that he had lost touch with those worlds. I thought that was very odd, too, because I imagined that the point of clubs was that no matter how often you went round the world and no matter how long, when you came back the club was there. However, as I only knew about clubs from the novels of Evelyn Waugh, I was prepared to believe that I was mistaken. In any case it also seemed that Rodney wanted particularly to belong to this author's sort of club, because he believed very strongly that one should do everything one did professionally and as he was now going to write books, he wanted to go to that sort of place.

"He's a strange fellow in many ways," Henry said, "a mass of contradictions." This didn't seem at all strange to me, because such people as I have met have all been a mass of contradictions. Nevertheless Rodney's particular contradiction in this case did seem odd to me. I had imagined that the whole point of his books would be that they should be thrown off in the midst of other activities —amateur productions that proved to be more brilliant than the professional. However, his new attitude if less romantic was more creditable and certainly more promising for Brodrick Layland. I decided indeed that he had probably only made this gesture to please Henry, which it did.

We dined once or twice with him and Lady Ann. She

has rather a nice house in Chester Square and he seemed
to be very comfortably installed—more permanently
indeed than his earlier talk of buying houses suggested.
However, this may well have been only the appearance
that Lady Ann gave to things, for she made every effort
short of absurdity to underline the nature of their relationship. I really could not blame her for this, for she
had made a catch that someone a good deal less battered
and ginny might have been proud of; and I had to admire
the manner in which she avoided the absurdity for, in fact,
looking at him and at her, it *was* very absurd, apart from
the large gap in their ages—fifteen years at least, I decided.

Lady Ann as usual talked most of the time. She has a
special way of being funny: she speaks with a drawl and a
very slight stutter and she ends her remarks suddenly
with a word or expression that isn't what one expects she
is going to lead up to. Well, of course, one does expect
it, because she always does it; and like a lot of things it
gets less funny when you've heard it a few times. For
example, she said she didn't agree with Rodney in not
liking *Look Back in Anger*, she'd been three times, the
music was so good. And again, she quite agreed with
Henry, she wouldn't have missed the Braque exhibition
for anything, but then she got a peculiar pleasure, almost
a sensual one, from being jammed really tight in a crowd.
And so on. Henry always laps up Lady Ann. She's a sort
of tarty substitute mother-figure for him, I think; and
indeed, if he wanted a tarty mother, he had to find a
substitute. I thought, perhaps, that Rodney would be a
little bored with her carry on, but if he was, he didn't
show it. This, of course, was very creditable of him, but

made me a little disappointed. Occasionally, it is true, he broke into the middle of her chatter; but then she interrupted him sometimes just as rudely. They might really have been a perfectly happy pair which I found even more disappointing.

I can't help thinking that by this time you may have formed some rather unfavourable views about the kind of woman I am. Well, I've already said that often I have very bitchy moods; and it's true, but at least I know it. But if you ask me why I have bitchy moods it's more difficult to say. In the first place life is frightfully boring nowadays, isn't it? And if you say I ought to try doing something with my time, well I have. I did translation from French and German for Brodrick Layland for a time; and I did prison visiting. They're quite different sorts of things to do and it didn't take long for me to get very bored with each of them. Not that I should want wars and revolutions—whenever there's an international crisis I get a ghastly pain in my stomach like everybody else. But, as I said, like England, I want security and I don't. However, what I was trying to explain about was my bitchy moods. Well, when I get very bored and depressed, I hate everyone and it seems to me everyone hates me. (As a matter of fact most people do like Henry better than me, although they think I'm more amusing.) But when the depressed moods lifts, I can't help feeling people are rather nice and they seem to like me too. I had these moods very badly when I was sixteen or so; and now in these last two years (since I was twenty-five) they've come back and they change much more quickly. When I talked to Henry about it once, he got so depressed and took such a 'psychological' view that I've never mentioned it again. In any case it's so easy to take 'psychological' views; but I'm by no means sure that it isn't just as true to say like my old nurse, "Well, we all have our ups and downs," and certainly that's a more cosy view of the situation.

But enough about me, because all this is really about Rodney Galt. Well, in those few times I saw him with Lady Ann (it seems more comic always to call her that) I began to have a theory about him; and when I get theories about people I get very interested in them. Especially as, if my theory was right, then Lady Ann and Henry and Mr Brodrick and no doubt lots of other people were liable to be sold all along the line or up the river or whatever the expression is; but on the whole, if my theory was right it only made *me* feel that he was *more* fascinating. The best sort of theory to have. One thing I did want to know more about was his family. In such cases I always believe in asking directly, so I said, "Where are your family, Rodney?" He smiled and said, "In the Midlothian where they've been for a sufficient number of recorded centuries to make them respectable. They're the best sort of people really," he added, "the kind of people who've always been content to be trout in the local minnow pond. I'm the only one who's shown the cloven hoof of fame-seeking. There must be a bounderish streak somewhere though not from mother's family who were all perfectly good dull country gentry. Of course, there was my great-great-great uncle the novelist. But his was a very respectable middling sort of local fame really."

Well there wasn't much given away there because after

all there are minnows and minnows and even 'country gentry' is rather a vague term. It was a bit disingenuous about Galt the novelist, because even I have heard of him and I know nothing of the Midlothian. And that was the chief annoyance, I knew absolutely no one with whom I could check up. But it didn't shake my theory.

Now we come to the most important point in this story: When Rodney Galt became our lodger. But first I shall have to explain about 'the lodger battle' which Henry and I had been then waging for over a year and this means explaining about our finances. Henry had some capital and he put that into Brodrick Layland and really, all things considered, he gets quite a good income back. But the house which we live in is mine; and it was left to me by my Aunt Agnes and it's rather a big house, situated in that vague area known as behind Harrod's. But it isn't, in fact, Pont Street Dutch. And in this big house there is only me and Henry and one or two foreign girls. They change usually every year and at the time I'm speaking of, about six or seven months ago, there was only one girl, a Swiss called Henriette Vaudoyer. Henry had long been keen that we should have a lodger who could have a bedroom and sitting-room and bathroom of their own. He said it was because he didn't like my providing the house and getting nothing back from it. He thought, that at least I ought to get pin money out of it. This was an absurd excuse because Daddy left me quite a little income—a great deal more than was required even if I were to set up a factory for sticking pins into wax images.

I think Henry had, at least, three real reasons for want-

ing this lodger; one, he thought it was wrong to have so
much space when people couldn't find anywhere to live,
and this, if I had thought of it first I would have agreed
with, because I have more social conscience really than
Henry, when I remember it; two, the empty rooms (empty
that is of human beings) reminded him of the tiny feet
that might have pattered but did not; three, he had an
idea that having a lodger would give me something to do
and help with the moods I've already told you about. The
last two of these reasons annoyed me very much and
made me very unwilling to have a lodger. So Henry was
rather shy in suggesting that we should let the top floor
to Rodney Galt. He only felt able to introduce the subject
by way of the brilliant first chapter of Rodney's new book.
Henry, it seemed, was bowled over by this chapter when
Rodney had submitted it and even Mr Brodrick, who had
his feet pretty firmly planted on the ground, rocked a
little. If it had been a feather in Henry's cap getting
Rodney Galt before, it became a whole plumage now.
Nothing must get in the way of the book's completion.
Well, it seemed that living at Lady Ann's did. Henry
pointed out that wonderful friend though Lady Ann was,
she could be difficult to live with if you wanted to write
because she talked so much. I said, yes, she did and drank
so much too. But I asked about the house that Rodney
was going to buy. Henry said that Rodney hadn't seen
the one he really wanted yet and he didn't want to do too
much house hunting while he was writing the book which
would require a lot of research. Above all, of course, he
did not want to involve himself with what might turn out
to be a white elephant. To this I thoroughly agreed. And,

to Henry's surprise and pleasure, I said, yes, Rodney could come as a lodger.

I was a little puzzled about Lady Ann. I made some enquiries and, as I suspected, Rodney had thrown her over and was said to have taken up with Susan Mullins, a very young girl but almost as rich as Lady Ann. However, Lady Ann was putting a good face on it before the world. I was glad to hear this because the face she usually put on before the world, although once good, was now rather a mess. But I didn't say anything to Henry about all this, because he was so fond of Lady Ann and I was feeling very friendly towards him for making such a sensible suggestion about a lodger.

Hardly had the lodger idea taken shape and Rodney was about to take up residence, when it almost lost its shape again. All because of Mr Brodrick. I should tell you that Henry's senior partner was again one of the many people about whom my mood varied. He was a rather handsome, grey-templed, port-flushed old man of sixty-five or so—more like a barrister than a publisher, one would think. Anyway what would one think a publisher looked like? He was a determinedly old-fashioned man—but not like Rodney, except that both of them talked a bit too much about wine and food. No, Mr Brodrick was an old world mannered, 'dear lady' sort of man—a widower who was gallant to the fair sex, is how he saw himself, I think. He had a single eyeglass on a black ribbon and ate mostly at his Club. Sometimes I thought he was rather a sweet old thing and sometimes I thought he was a ghastly old bore and a bit common to boot.

At first, it seemed, he'd been delighted at Henry's capturing Rodney for their list, mainly because he was rather an old snob and Rodney seemed to know well a lot of people whom he himself had only met once or twice but talked about a good deal. He patted Henry on the back once or twice—literally I imagine though not heartily—and saw him even more as "a son, my dear boy, since I have not been blessed with any offspring myself". (I often wondered whether Mr Brodrick didn't say to Henry, "When's the baby coming along?" He was so keen on heirs for Brodrick Layland.)

But suddenly it seemed that one day Mr Brodrick was talking to Mr Harkness of Harkness & Co, and Mr Harkness said that why they hadn't gone on with Rodney as an author was because they'd had a lot of financial trouble with him—loans not repaid and so on. Mr Brodrick didn't care for the sound of that at all and he thought that they should do what he called "Keeping a very firm rein on Master Galt's activities". And as he saw Henry as a son and perhaps me as a daughter-in-law (who knows?) he was very much against our having Rodney as a lodger. The more strictly commercial the relations with authors the better, he said.

Henry was upset by all this and a good deal surprised at what Mr Harkness had said. I was not at all surprised but I did not say so. I said that Harkness had no right to say such things and Mr Brodrick to listen to them. In any case, I said, how did we know that Mr Harkness had not just made them up out of sour grapes. And as to commercial relations I pointed out that Rodney's being a lodger was commercial and anyway the rent was being paid to me. So Mr Brodrick knew what he could do. But Henry still seemed a little unhappy and then he told me that he had himself lent Rodney various sums. So then I saw there was nothing for it but the brilliant first chapter —and I played that for all I was worth. Did Henry, I said, expect that anyone capable of that brilliant first chapter was going to fit in with every bourgeois maxim of life that people like Harkness and Mr Brodrick laid down in their narrow scheme of things? I was surprised, I said, that Henry who had a real flair for publishing because he cared about books should be led into this sort of 'business is business' attitude that, if persevered in, would mean confining one's list to all the dullest books produced. Anyway I made it clear I was determined that Rodney Galt should come if only as a matter of principle. When Henry saw that I was determined, he decided to stand on principle too and on the great coup he had made for Brodrick Layland as forecast by that brilliant first chapter. So Rodney moved in.

What with all the research Rodney needed to do for his book and what with Susan Mullins you may think that I was getting unduly excited about nothing. But if you have jumped to that conclusion, well then I think you can't have a very interesting mind and you certainly don't understand me. When I say that I had become interested in Rodney that's exactly what I mean and 'being interested' with me comes to this—that I don't know really what I want or indeed if I want anything at all, but I know for certain that I don't want to leave go. So for the first week or so Rodney went to the British Museum and read books about civility and honour of which they have lots there—

intended when they were published in the seventeenth
and eighteenth century for people who were on the social
make, I think. I rather used to like to think that after all
this time they were being read again by Rodney. When
he was not at the British Museum, he was with Susan
Mullins or on the telephone talking to her.

The British Museum fell out of Rodney's life before
Susan Mullins. After only a fortnight it was replaced by
books from the London Library which as Rodney had a
sitting-room seemed only sensible. Then came a period
when Susan did not telephone so often and once or twice
Rodney telephoned to her and spoke instead to her
mother (who was not called Mullins but Lady Newnham
because she had been divorced and married again to a
very rich Conservative industrialist peer) and then high
words were exchanged. And finally one day when he
rang he spoke to Lord Newnham and very high words
were exchanged and that was the end of that. It became
difficult then for Rodney to keep his mind even on the
books from the London Library let alone going to the
British Museum. It seemed somehow that his mind was
diverted more by financial schemes than by study. None
of this surprised me much either, but I thought I would
not worry Henry by telling him in case he began to be
afraid that there would only be a brilliant first chapter and
no more. In any case it might have only been temporary,
though I was not inclined to think that.

So Rodney and I used to go out in his MG (and perhaps
it would have been more in keeping if he had refused to
use any kind of motor-car later than a De Dionne but I
was glad that he didn't.) We went here, there and every-

where and all over the place. We saw a great number of lovely houses—a lot in London, but gradually more and more outside London. Rodney came very near to taking some of them, he said. And then since he proposed to turn some of the houses when he bought them into furnished rooms or flats, we looked at a great number of antiques. The antiques we looked at were rather expensive for this purpose, but Rodney said that only good things interested him and what was the good of his expertise if he never used it. But it was quite true—that he had expertise, I mean. We also had a lot of very good luncheons. On my theory Rodney would pay for these during the first phase, but later I expected I would have to pay. But I was determined to make the first phase last as long as possible and I succeeded. We took to going suddenly too to places like Hampton Court and Cambridge and Hatfield House and Wilton. We did not go to see any friends, though, partly because it wouldn't have done, but mostly because we really were very content to be alone together. However, often when we passed great parks or distant large houses, Rodney told me to which of his friends they belonged; and this was nice for him.

In fact we both had a wonderful time, although Rodney's time would have been more wonderful, he said, if I'd agreed to go to bed with him. Sometimes he cajoled; or at least he made himself as attractive and sweet as he could which was a lot; and this, I imagine, is what 'cajole' means. But often he took a very high-handed line, because in Rodney's theory of seducing there was a lot about women wanting to be mastered which fitted into his general social views. Then he would tell me that unless I let myself go and accepted his mastery which was what I really wanted, I would soon become a tight little bitch. I had, he said, all the makings of one already at twenty-six. "You think," he cried, "that because you have attractive eyes and a good figure that you can go on having sex appeal just by cock-teasing every man you meet. But let me tell you it won't last, you'll quickly become a hard little bitch that no one will be interested in. It's happening already with your bitter humour and your whimsy and your melancholy moods. You're ceasing to be 'civilised'." Civilisation seemed to be his key to seduction, because he made light of my married position on the same grounds. "In any civilised century," he said, "the situation would be sensibly accepted," and then he talked of Congreve and Vanbrurgh and Italian society. But I didn't care to decide too easily, because Vanbrurgh and Congreve are no longer alive and this is not Italy of the Cicisbei and affairs of this kind aren't easy to control and even if life was often boring it was secure. Also I quite enjoyed things as they were, even the violent things he said about my becoming a bitch, but I wasn't sure that I would like all that masterfulness on a physical plane.

So we went on as I wished and I enjoyed managing the double life and if Rodney didn't exactly enjoy it he was very good at it. For example, one morning an absolutely ghastly thing happened; Henry's mother suddenly arrived as Rodney and I were about to set off for Brighton. I have already said about Henry's mother that you can feel two ways about her; I think that I would be prepared to feel the nicer way more often if she didn't seem to feel so consistently the nastier way about me. As it is, our relations are not very good and as, like most people, we find it easier to fight battles on our home grounds, we don't often meet.

Henry's mother doesn't bother much about dress and that day being a rather cold summer day she was wearing an old squirrel-skin coat over her tweeds. As to her hats, you can never tell much about these, because her grey hair gets loose so much and festoons all over them. It is said in the Raven family that she should have been allowed by her father to go to the University and that she would then have been a very good scholar and happy to be so. As it is, she has lived most of her life in a large red-brick Queen Anne house in Hampshire and the only way that you can tell that she is not happy like all the other ladies is that as well as gardening and jam making and local government, she does all the very difficult cross-word puzzles very quickly and as well as the travel books and biographies recommended in the Sunday papers she reads sometimes in French and even in German. She closed her eyes when she saw me but this was no especial insult because as I have said she always does this when she speaks.

"You shouldn't live so close to Harrod's, June dear, if you don't want morning callers," was how she greeted me.

As Rodney and I were both obviously about to go out there was not much to answer to this. But the Ravens have a habit of half-saying what is on their minds and it immediately seemed certain to me that she had only come there because she'd heard about the lodger and wanted to pry. I said, "This is Rodney Galt, our lodger. This is Henry's mother."

Rodney must have formed the same conclusion for he immediately said, "How do you do? I'm afraid this is a very brief meeting because I'm just off to the London Library."

"Oh?" Henry's mother answered. "You must be one of those new members who have all the books out when one wants them. It's so difficult being a country member. Of course, when Mr Cox was alive," and she sighed, putting the blame on to Rodney but also making it quite clear to me that it was him she wanted to investigate. I thought it would be wise to deflect her so I said, "You'll stay and have a coffee or a drink or something, won't you?"

But she was not to be deflected. "What strange ideas you have about how I spend my mornings, June dear," she answered, "I haven't come up from Kingston, you know. I'm afraid you're one of those busy people who think everybody idle but yourself. I just thought it would be proper since I was so close at Harrods that we should show each other that we were both still alive. But I don't intend to waste your time, dear. Indeed if Mr Galt is going to the London Library I think I shall ask him if he will share a taxi with me. I'm getting a little old to be called 'duckie' as these bus ladies seem to like to do now."

So Rodney was caught good and proper. However, I needn't have worried for him, because when Henry came home I learned that his mother had been round to Brodrick Layland and had spent her time singing Rodney's praises. It appeared that he'd been so helpful in finding her the best edition of Saint Simon that she had offered him luncheon and that he had suggested Wheelers. His conversation must have been very pleasing to her for she made no grumble about the bill. She had only said to Henry, "I can't think why you described him as a beautiful-looking young man. He's most presentable and very well informed too." So we seemed to have got over that hurdle.

But Rodney was a success with all our friends; for example, with 'les jeunes filles en fleur'. This is the name that Henry and I give to two ladies called Miss Jackie Reynolds and Miss Marcia Railton and the point about the name is that although like Andrée and Albertine, they are Lesbian ladies, they are by no means jeunes filles and certainly not en fleur. Henry is very fond of them because like Lady Ann they make him feel broadminded. They are very generous and this is particularly creditable because they do not make much money out of their business of interior decoration. They have lived together for a great many years—since they were young indeed which must be a great, great many years ago—and Henry always says that this is very touching. Unfortunately they are often also very boring and this seems to be all right for Henry, because when they have been particularly boring, he remembers how touching their constancy to each other is and this apparently compensates him. But it doesn't compensate me.

When the jeunes filles met Rodney, Jackie who is short and stocky with an untidy black-dyed shingle, put her head on one side and said, "I say, isn't he a smasher!" And Marcia who is petite rather than stocky and alto-

gether dainty in her dress, said, "But of a Beauty!" This
is the way they talk when they meet new people; Henry
says it's because they are shy, and so it may be, but it
usually makes everybody else rather shy too. I thought it
would paralyse Rodney, but he took it in his stride and
said, "Oh! come, I'm not as good-looking as all that."
That was when I first realised that I preferred Rodney on
his own and this in itself is a difficulty because if one is
going to be much with somebody you are bound to be
with other people sometimes. However, the evening
went swimmingly. Rodney decided that, although he
would always have really good objects in his *own* house,
the people to whom he let furnished flats would be much
happier to be interior decorated and who better to do it
than les jeunes filles en fleur? Well, that suited Marcia
and Jackie all right. They got together, all three in a
huddle, and a very funny huddle it was. Rodney already
knew of some Americans, even apart from all the people
who would be taking furnished flats from him when he
had them to offer, and the rest of the evening was spent
in deal discussions. Henry said afterwards he'd never felt
so warm to Rodney as when he saw how decent he was to
les jeunes filles. I wasn't quite sure what the decency
meant but still . . .

The truth was that much though I was enjoying
Rodney's company, I was beginning to get a little depressed by the suit he was so ardently pressing and the
decision that this ardour was forcing upon me. It would
be so much nicer if there was no cause and effect in life,
no one thing leading inevitably to another, but just everything being sufficient in itself. But I could see that

F

Rodney was not the kind of person to take life in this way and quite suddenly something forced this realisation upon me rather strongly.

I have not said much about our Swiss, Henriette Vaudoyer, and I don't propose to say much now because nothing is more boring than talk about foreign domestics. I have to put up with it at three-quarters of the dinners we go to. Henriette was a very uninteresting girl, but quite pretty. There were only four of us in the house: Henry and me in one bedroom and Rodney and Henriette in two bedrooms. Well, no one can be surprised that Rodney and Henriette began to be in one bedroom sometimes too. I wasn't surprised but I was upset, it gave me a pain in my stomach. Clearly there were only two things I could do about that pain: get rid of Rodney or get rid of Henriette. The brave thing would have been to get rid of Rodney before I got worse pains; but already the pain was so bad that I was not brave enough. I gave Henriette notice. She said some very unpleasant, smug, Swiss sort of things to me and she began to say them to Henry which was more worrying. Luckily one of Henry's great virtues is that he never listens to tale-bearing and he did what is called 'cut her short'. However, he was a bit worried that I should decide to be without a foreign girl, because we'd always had one and sometimes two. But I explained that we had Mrs Golfin coming in, and she was only too pleased to come in even more, and for the rest, having more to do would be wonderful for my moods about which I was getting worried. So Henry saw the necessity and Henriette went. But I saw clearly too that I would have to decide either to accept Rodney's importuning or not, because soon he would take no answer as the same as "answer—no".

I think maybe I might have answered no, only at the time Henry annoyed me very much over the holiday question. This is a very old and annoying question with us. Every year since we were married Henry says, "Well, I don't know why we shouldn't manage Venice (or Madrid, or Rome) this year. I think we've deserved it." And first, I want to say that people don't deserve holidays, they just take them; and secondly, I want to point out that we're really quite rich and there's no question of our not being able to 'manage' Venice or Rome. I long, in fact, for the day when he will say, "Well, I don't know why we shouldn't manage Lima this year, taking in Honolulu and Madagascar on the way home." But if he can't say that—and he can't—then I would prefer him to ask, "Shall we go to Italy or Spain or North Africa this year, June? The choice is yours." However, just about the time that Henriette left, he came out with it. "Well, I don't see why we shouldn't manage Florence this year." So I said, "Well I do, Henry, because I don't bloody well want to go there." And then he was very upset and as I was feeling rather guilty anyway, I apologised and said how silly my moods were and Florence would be rather enchanting.

Henry cheered up a good deal at this. "If that is so," he said, "I'm very glad, because it makes it much easier for me to tell you something. It's been decided on the spur of the moment that I'm to go to New York on business. It's only for a fortnight but I must leave next week."

Now I wouldn't really have wanted to go to New York for Brodrick Layland on a rush visit but somehow everything conspired together to make me furious and I decided then and there that what I wanted was what Rodney wanted, physical mastery or no. And actually when the time came, the physical mastery wasn't such a trial. I mean there was nothing 'extra' or worrying about it. And for the rest, I was very pleased.

So that when Henry set off for New York, I was committed on a new course of life, as they say. But the weekend before Henry left, he insisted on running me down to a country hotel in Sussex and making a fuss of me. I suppose I should have felt very bad about it, because really he did his best to make the fuss as good as possible. But all I could think of was that I did hope cause and effect and one thing following another wasn't going to make life worse instead of better. After all I had made this committal to a new course in order to make life *less* boring, but if it meant that there were going to be more decisions and choices in front of me, it would be much *more* boring. One thing, however, I *did* decide was that I would try not to talk about Rodney to Henry even if I did have to think of him. After all, talking about Rodney would not have been a very kind return for the fussing.

In the end, however, it was Henry who raised the subject of Rodney. It seemed that Lady Ann had not been able to put a good face on all the time. One day at a cocktail party when even she had found the gin stronger than usual she had dropped her face in front of Henry. She said that the money she had spent on Rodney nobody knew—this I thought was hypocritical because she was just telling Henry how much it was—and the return he'd made had been beneath anything she'd ever experienced. I must say she couldn't have said worse, considering the sort of life she's led. Henry was very upset, because although he liked Rodney, Lady Ann was such a very old friend. But I said that age in friendship was not the proper basis for judgment (after all just because Lady Ann was so old!) and I also reminded him that hell had no fury. I succeeded in pacifying him because he didn't want his fussing of me to be spoiled, but I could see that things would never be the same between Rodney and Henry, as now indeed they were not between any of the three of us.

Well, there we were—Rodney and me alone for ten days. And Rodney did exactly the right thing—he suggested that we spent most of the time in Paris. How right this was! First there was the note of absurdity of adultery in Paris. "That," said Rodney, "should satisfy your lack of self-assurance. Your passion to put all your actions in inverted commas." It must be said that Rodney, for someone only my age, understands me very well, because I do feel less troubled about doing anything when I can see it as faintly absurd. Of course, the reasons he gives don't satisfy me very well; when I asked him why I was like that, he said, "Because you're incurably middle class, June darling." On the whole though, by this time Rodney gave me less of his 'patrician line'. However, things had not yet reached the pass that I could tell Rodney my theory about him.

This theory, you will already have guessed, was that he

was little better or little worse or whatever than an adventurer, not to say, a potential crook. I did indeed know that his affairs had reached a serious state because of some of the telephone conversations that I overheard and because of the bills that kept arriving. The nicest thing was that Rodney paid the whole of the Paris trip. It is true that he hadn't paid for his rent for some weeks; it is also true that his trip to Paris was intended as an investment; nevertheless I think it was very lovely of him to have paid the Paris trip when he was up to his eyes in debts. Let me say that until the last day or so the Paris trip was everything I could ask or that money could buy. Also, though I don't think Rodney realised this, it was a great relief to me not to be committing adultery in Henry's house (for in a sense it *was* Henry's although it belonged to me).

It was only the last day but one of our trip, when we were sitting at a café looking at the Fontainbleau twiddly staircase and drinking Pernod that Rodney began to press his further suit. I had been expecting it, of course; indeed it was the choice that lay ahead, the inevitable decision, and all the other things that I had so hoped would not happen but that I knew would. He asked me, in fact, to leave Henry for him. At first he just said it was what we both wanted. Then he said he loved me too much to see me go on living with Henry in such a dead, pretence life, getting more bitterly whimsical and harder every year. Then he said I was made like him to use life up and enjoy people and things and then pass on to others. It was all very unreal; but if he had only known it was exactly this confidence trick part of him that attracted me. I could quite clearly see the life of travel and hotels we should have on my money and the bump there would be when we got through my money which I think Rodney would have done rather quickly. But it was the bogusness, the insecurity and even perhaps the boue beneath for which I had such a nostalgie.

Somehow, however, he didn't grasp this or perhaps he was too anxious to secure his aims. For he suddenly changed his tone and became a pathetic, dishonest little boy pleading for a chance. He was desperate, he said, and it must look as though he was after my money, for he was sure I had put two and two together. This I had to admit. "Well," he said, "then you know the worst." But he begged me to believe if he could have me with him, it would be different. He had real talent and he only needed some support to use it. Did I understand, he asked me, exactly what his life had been? And then he told me of his background—his father was a narrow, not very successful builder in a small Scotch town—he described to me most movingly his hatred of it all, his hard if dishonest fight to get into a different world, the odds against him. It was I, he begged, who could get him on to the tram-lines again.

I don't think I'm very maternal really, because I didn't find myself moved; I only felt cheated. If I hadn't been sure that in fact whatever he said, life with Rodney would have been much more like what I imagined than what he was now promising, I should have turned him down on the spot. As it was I said I must think about it. He must leave me alone in London for at least a fortnight and then I would give him an answer. He accepted this because anyway he had business in France, so I returned to London alone.

Henry was glad on his return to find Rodney absent, I think. And in a short while he was even more glad still. Or, at any rate, I was, because if Rodney had been in our house I think that Henry would have hit him. This, of course, might have fitted into Rodney's ideas of the violence of life, even if not into his view of civilisation; and probably Rodney being much younger he would have won the fight, which would have made me very angry because of Henry. But it is just possible that Henry would have won and this would have made me very sad because of my ideal picture of Rodney.

What put the lid on it (as they used to say at some period which I'm not sure of the date of) for Henry was a visit he made to his mother shortly after his return, when he discovered that Rodney had borrowed money from her. I could only think that if Rodney could get money from Henry's mother he had little to fear about the future (and maybe if my future was joined to his, though precarious, it would not founder). But Henry, of course, saw it differently and so did I, when I heard of the sum involved which was only £50, a sum of money insufficient to prevent foundering.

Hardly had Henry's mother dealt Henry's new-found friendship a blow from the right, when up came les jeunes filles and dealt it a knockout from the left. It seemed that they had busily decorated and furnished two flats for American friends of Rodney's—one for Mrs Milton Brothers and one for Robert J. Masterson and family— and as these American people were visiting the Continent before settling in England, the bills had been given to Rodney to send to them. The bills were quite large because Rodney had told les jeunes filles not to cheese-pare. Now Mrs Brothers and Mr Masterson and family had arrived in London and it seemed that they had already given the money for les jeunes filles to Rodney plus his commission. Jackie said, "You can imagine what it makes us look like," and Marcia said, "Yes, really it *is* pretty grim." Then Jackie said, "We look such awful chumps," and that I think was what I agreed with most. Henry said he felt sure that when Rodney returned, he would have some explanation to offer. I didn't think this likely and I didn't think Henry did. "Well," said Jackie, "that's just it. I'm not sure that Rodney ought to return because if Mrs Brothers goes on as she is now, I think there'll be a warrant out for him soon."

I felt miserable when they had gone and so did Henry, but for different reasons. All I could find to do was to pray that Mrs Brothers should die in her bath before she could start issuing warrants. Henry said, "I only hope he doesn't come near this house again, because I'm not sure what my duty would be."

Then, the very next morning, at about eleven o'clock the telephone rang and it *was* Rodney. I told him what Henry had said and we agreed that it was most important that he should come to the house when Henry was out. He came, in fact, just before lunch.

I had expected him to look a little haunted like Humphrey Bogart sometimes used to in fugitive films; he did look a little hunted but it wasn't quite like the films. Less to my taste. As I looked at him, I suddenly thought of something. So I made an excuse and ran upstairs and hid my jewel box. I would have hated to have been issuing warrants for Rodney. Then when we had a long chat and something more. About that I will only say I have rather a "time and a place" view and so it ended things as far as I was concerned with a whimper rather than a bang. As to the chat, I said that I had thought things over and the answer was no, very reluctantly. And when people say "you don't know what it cost me", I think it's rather stupid because they could always tell you. So I will tell what this cost me—it cost me the whole of a possible, different life with someone very attractive. I shall always regret it when the life I am leading is particularly boring, which it often is. But that, after all, is the nature of decisions. The answer had to be no. And I do not despair of other chances. But life is, indeed, a cheat.

What Rodney said after my negative answer was a pity. He went on again about how soon I would become a hard little bitch and rather depressing with all my 'amusing' talk. He even said, "I should think you might go off your head. People who get the idea that they can make a game of other people's lives often do."

I must say that I thought, everything considered about Rodney's own life, this was a bit too much. And in any case all this toughness and bullying was all right when Rodney was pressing his suit, but now that the suit had been pressed and sent back, I thought it all rather boring. And so I changed the conversation to the warrant that might be out at any moment. Rodney was well aware of this, he said, and he had almost enough but not quite to get abroad that night. I said I would see what I could find in ready cash, because obviously cheques would be no good. He didn't seem sure about this, but I stuck to my point, emphasising how little he understood money matters as evidenced in his life.

While I was looking for what cash I had, he went upstairs to the lavatory and I heard him walking about in my bedroom so I was glad for his sake that I had hidden my jewel box. And I did find enough to help him overseas, because I had put some aside in case he turned up, although I did not tell him this. Away, looking rather hunted but still very handsome, he went out of my life.

It was all rather an anti-climax without Rodney, although his name was kept alive, what with Henry's mother, and les jeunes filles, and the Americans, and Mr Brodrick furious at only having a first chapter, however brilliant, after paying so much in advances. But all this was not the same for me as Rodney's physical presence, not at all the same.

It was only a month later that it got into the papers in quite a small column that he'd been arrested for stealing some money at the house of the Marchesa Ghirlaindini in Rome where he was a guest. It mentioned also about Mrs Brother's warrant.

Well, I did miss the excitement of life with him and the decision that I hated so much when I had to make it; so I got talking to an old friend of mine—Mary Mudie who writes a long, gossipy column in a Sunday newspaper. And sure enough there was a featured bit about him the very next Sunday. All about the well-known people he'd dined with and about Lady Ann Denton, how he was one of the "many fortunate young men of talent and charm who had profited by her friendship", and how valuable she was as a bridge between her generation and the young. Then there was a bit about Rodney's great brilliance as a writer and how few who knew him in this capacity realised his double life. It told us with what expectancy connoisseurs of the fresh and original in modern writing had awaited his new book and how ironic its title *Honour and Civility* now seemed. So brilliant was the first chapter of this, it said, that an old established publishing firm, famed for its cautious policy, had gone to unusual lengths to assist its young author. Realising the supreme importance to a writer of congenial surroundings in which to work, the enterprising junior partner Mr Henry Raven even installed their brilliant protégé as a tenant in his own house. Then came a block heading "More Friend than Lodger" and it was followed by a bit about me. " 'I can hardly believe that Rodney was leading this double life,' said almond-eyed, brunette June Raven, well-known young London hostess and wife of publisher Raven, 'he was more of a friend than a lodger as far as I was concerned. He was not only clever and witty, but he had the rare gift of easy intimacy.' " Dear Mary followed this up immediately with a mention of Rodney's first book, *Cuckoo*—a study of married infidelity in history's pages as witty as it was scholarly." The paragraphs went on with a little interview with Rodney's parents. " 'Rodney never took to the building trade,' his father told me in the front parlour of his typical unpretentious little Scots 'hame', 'he always wanted big things out of life.' " And then Mary ended on a moral note, "Rodney Galt got his big things—bigger perhaps than he imagined when an Italian court on Monday last sentenced him. . . ." It was a sad little article, but I did think it was clever of Mary to have made so much of what I told her.

I'm afraid Rodney will be very upset by the piece about his parents, but he did say very nasty things to me. And Henry, too, won't like the "more friend than lodger" part, but Henry ought to pay for my being faithful to him too, I think. At least that's how I feel, after life has presented me with such awful choices.

Sure enough Henry read Mary's article and got into a terrible rage. "I'm pretty sure it's actionable," he said. So I looked very nonchalant and said, "I don't think so, darling, because I supplied Mary with all the information." Then he looked at me and said, "I think you should be very careful, June, this sort of mischievous behaviour is frequently a danger signal. It may seem a strange thing to say to you but you'd only have yourself to blame if you went off your head." He was trembling when he went out of the room, so I think it likely that he'd known about me and Rodney for some time.

Well, there you are—both Henry and Rodney take a 'psychological' view of me. But as I said before I often think that common sense views are wiser. I spoke before of my old nurse and what she used to say of me was, "Miss June wants to have her cake and eat it." Well, so do most people one meets nowadays. But I think perhaps I want it more than the rest, which make me think that in the end I'll get it.

Once a Lady

EILEEN CARTER tightened the cord of her sandy Jaeger dressing-gown around her full waist, for the routine of preparing for bed was a lengthy one, and her pink and white striped boy's flannel pyjamas were loose and inclined, when not controlled, to impede her actions. Habitual though all the preparation was, she went at it doggedly, her heavy face—a rosy-cheeked bulldog's—set in childish concentration. First she heated the milk in the little suacepan on the spirit stove in the corner of her bedroom; then she poured three dessertspoons of whisky into the milk. She placed the milk with two Marie biscuits on her bedside-table with her reading glasses, her sleeping pills and *The Cloud of Unknowing* (Mrs Underhill's translation). Then she knelt beside her bed and said The Lord's Prayer. Once in bed, she kicked the hot bottle to rest at her feet, slowly drank the milk and ate both biscuits, while she read from the book. "All men will they reprove of their defaults, right as they had cure of their souls; and yet they think that they do not else for God, unless they tell him their defaults that they see. And they say that they be stirred thereto by the fire of charity, and of God's love in their hearts: and truly they lie, for it is with the fire of hell welling in their brains and in their imagination." But the passage seemed inapposite to her this night. She had of course been guilty of moral righteousness and censoriousness in the past—often and often—lonely people, she reflected are prone to this sin, but at this moment she only wished to dwell on one person's virtues, to give praise to the one she loved. And this, too, was sin also to which lonely people were prone. She tried to deflect her mind by reading other passages, but the obtrusive thoughts kept breaking in. She was not unaware that the Devil sometimes increased his power by forcing his victims to fight him, but rather in withdrawal lay victory; she, therefore, put by her book, put off her dressing-gown and, taking a small green pill with the last drains of the milk, prepared for sleep. It came quickly, but just before she slept she saw Esther's dear face smiling at her and she smiled lovingly in return.

Far across the village, over the pond, and the pub and the crescent of new council houses, in the big bedroom above the shop, Esther Barrington lay awake beside her husband Jim. Esther was used now to waking suddenly in the night, sometimes from alarming dreams, sometimes just from nothing, but always appallingly and hopelessly awake. To-night she tried, as so often, to attribute her wakefulness to the screech-owl that settled on the telegraph wire above the outside lavatory and watched the chickens in their sleep. She blamed it upon the sudden stirrings of young jackdaws in the roof eaves. She was tempted to wake Jim from his heavy sleep and tell him it was all his fault—for despite his deep sleeping he constantly turned and muttered. When the despair at

being awake became urgent, she thought of getting up
and running into Mother's room and telling her it was
her fault for having become senile and for moaning sense-
lessly in the night. 'You're not my mother,' she thought
to shout at her. 'Just because you stood by Jim and me
'at the time', doesn't mean that we have to support you
for ever. You must leave.' But how could a semi-
paralysed old woman of seventy leave? In any case, this
hysterical attempt to put the blame on others did not last
long, for her very wakefulness seemed to come from so
deep within her that it pushed out everything except con-
sciousness of herself. She could think of nothing, see
nothing, feel nothing but herself awake.

She tried desperately to force some issue—some
thoughts, or at the least, some memory—out of this
blank selfness. In the years before, when she had not
been drained by work and futility, she had been able to
imagine and think with willed concentration—curiously
able for one with only a genteel girl's education. Now
memory came only in flashed pictures that jolted shakily
before her eyes as from a badly operated magic lantern,
trembled there for a moment and then flicked out as
though the electricity had failed. As for thoughts, they
led nowhere.

She heard Mother moaning in the next room, and told
herself that it was just child's crying, with no more meaning than that; and then she set herself to reflect whether
indeed a child's crying meant so little, whether its terrors
were indeed so transitory. Her mind, however, would
make nothing of it. Scenes of her own childhood misery,
of the cupboard in the vicarage nursery where she had

taken her sorrows, or of the dank, rotting-leaved ground behind the hibiscus where she had fled grown-up solicitude, came before her sharply and were as sharply gone. And then, as though flashed on the local cinema screen— the old, tedious generalities. *You* have no children; It's worked out badly; Perhaps I'm to blame, I'm to blame, I'm tired of it all. She heard in recollection Lottie Washington's dismal droning next door, "Oh, I never felt more like crying all night, for everything's wrong and nothing ain't right." Then, defeated by the fact that all her attempts at thinking had ended only in recollection of a vulgar popular song, she turned to doing sums in her head. After all her true anxieties were practical. She went over the biscuit orders they had placed, did the confectionery accounts and measured the dwindling returns from egg sales against the possible returns from homemade jam; but everything always depended on bills and figures that lay downstairs in the sawdusty, soapy-smelling dark of the shop. Past accounts now came into her head, and the large sums that had once spelt the failure of their farming venture became inextricably involved with the little bills of the shop that now kept their heads just above water. She saw herself and Jim swimming in the waterfilled shop, their heads bobbing up and down like ducks, she thought indignantly—an *absurd* position for a woman who had once given scandal to her family, a woman who had married beneath her for love, a woman who had stolen another woman's husband. She checked a sudden loud laugh as she realised to what novelettish terms she had reduced the central action of her life. The laughter turned to bitter sobbing, which in turn she

G

checked. She had no right to add to Jim's already cruelly heavy day by disturbing his sleep.

The church clock sounded four. "I'm not a bit tired," she said to herself, "sleeplessness is only harmful if you allow yourself to think it so." She knew, however, how tired she would be when the alarm sounded at half-past five. And now to calm her came the reflection which increasingly supported her resolution to hold on. It took great courage for someone brought up as I was to do what I did. She hated the snobbish implication of the thought; nevertheless she moved away from Jim in the bed and pride at her reflection gave her calm.

Polly Washington had climbed over the fence and was talking to the hens. Since Miss Cleaver had taken her up in Sunday School, teaching her little poems to recite and encouraging her to make up little dances for herself, she had become so ladylike and hardly played with the other village children any more.

She was for ever picking little bunches of flowers and holding little conversations with the animals. At first Lottie and Reg Washington had encouraged her and made her show off her dance in a little peach silk party frock every Sunday afternoon to visitors. After a while they had lost patience with her little whimsies; Lottie was too busy to have a child hanging round all day; and even old Granny Washington had slapped her and called her "a little madam". She spent more and more of her time now at the Barringtons, following Esther round with stories or giving 'pretence presents' to old Mrs Barrington who was too senile to grasp that they were not real and said, "Thank you, my dear," so that the little girl broke into giggles.

"Good morning, Mrs Speckly Hen," Polly said to the Plymouth Rock fowl, in the special puking, ladylike little voice that Miss Cleaver had taught her to use for pretending games.

Esther had already given Jim his breakfast and had sent him out on the milk round for Clarkson's before she came out into the dust blowing October gale to feed the hens. It was one of Jim's jobbing gardening days and she had sandwiches to cut for him as well as the usual chores—beds to make, Mother to put on the commode—before she opened the shop. Gusts of cold wind blew up her sleeves, licked round her legs, reminding her of the approaching winter she so dreaded. How long would Jim's obstinacy refuse to accept that the fowls—last sentimental relic of their farm's high hopes—added nothing but trouble to their lives?

"Good morning, Mrs Barrington," Polly said in a special sweet voice. Miss Cleaver had told her that she must always be a very kind, polite little girl to poor pretty little Mrs Barrington.

Esther started into recognition of the child's presence with irritation. Polly round her feet at seven o'clock in the morning! There seemed to be no hour at which those wretched people cared for their offspring. Did the child get no breakfast? They trade on the weakness of my barrenness, she thought bitterly.

"Good morning, Polly," she said, "and a very busy morning for everybody." The hard lines that now lay beneath the soft surface of her pretty, little bird-like face snapped into place as she spoke.

"*My* mummy isn't busy," Polly answered, "she's listening to the wireless."

Esther made no reply as she forced open the rickety fowl-house door and fought her way through the acrid-smelling, clucking birds. Polly ran excitedly behind her, increasing the hens' alarms, getting in the way of the scattering corn. "Mrs Speckley Hen had a dream last night, Mrs Barrington," she cried and she paused, her face red and bursting with imaginative effort, for, despite all Miss Cleaver's encouragement, she was a girl of very limited fancy. "She dreamt she laid a big, big, big chocolate egg," she said triumphantly. "Oh look, look, Mrs Barrington, there's the greedy one with the little yellow patch on her foot. What shall we call her? Mrs Yellow Patch?"

"I haven't time to give hens names this morning, Polly."

From over the hedge Esther could hear Lottie Washington's droning, 'I never felt so like singing the blues.' Out of the corner of her eye she saw the cigarette dangling from Lottie's fresh, full mouth, her lazy, easy, sensual movements as she reached up to fix the clothes pegs on the line. "You *must* not come over here so early, Polly," Esther said loudly and sternly. Lottie immediately called raucously, "Polly, Polly, come back here at once."

"I'm sorry, Mrs Washington," Esther said, "I cannot have Polly here at all hours of the day."

Lottie did not answer, but as the little girl scrambled red-faced over the hedge, she caught her by the arm,

twisted it and slapped her face. "Don't you go where
you're not wanted," she said and pushed the crying child
towards the back door. Esther scattered the last of the
corn, shut the hen-house door and returned indoors,
feeling a little sick.

She was already behind the counter serving or rather
listening to old Mrs Sumper, when Jim returned from his
milk round. "She were like a little sleeping child as she
lay there. Doctor said 'e'd never seen one go so peaceful,
not as 'ad gone with the cancer."

Through the old woman's words, Esther saw her
husband for a moment as a stranger entering the shop.
Swarthily handsome, strong but gentle; a strong, steady
face set in heavy lines of patience. People said that she
too had kept her prettiness. And as to the lines they only
gave more interest to the face, people said. Well, let them
say; that was all right if every line didn't speak of past
worries and of back-breaking labours. As to the gentleness and patience, if only she didn't resent them. He
ought to be more angry, more resentful, she thought, I've
cheated him and he ought to hate me for it   What does
love mean if it breeds only gentleness? She indicated
his sandwiches to him, but he only smiled and went
upstairs.

When he came down again Mrs Sumper had finished
her story. "Well, there it is," she said, "you haven't got
'em so I'll have to get 'em at Rayners' when I go into
Lichfield Saturday." She sniffed resentfully and waddled
out of the shop.

"Mother's waiting for her breakfast," Jim said.

"Oh, Jim," Esther cried, "she's *had* her breakfast, I gave it to her half an hour ago."

"Ah! The poor old thing's forgotten then."

"Well, she really shouldn't have done. I gave her two sardines and she insisted on dipping them into her tea." For some reason, Esther heard herself laugh loudly.

Jim's dark, calf's eyes looked sadly hurt for a moment, then, "You've got enough to do without extra burdens," he said, "we'll have to send her away."

It annoyed her that after fifteen years of married life with her, peasant fears and ignorance showed through his good sense and independence in phrases like "send her away". She admired him still so much that it enraged her to think of his humility before authorities like hospitals or doctors. He had been so meek and uncomplaining three years ago when the failure of the farm had ended in two bouts of pneumonia.

"Don't be silly, Jim, we've discussed all that," she said, and she began bustling about behind the counter rearranging tins on the shelves. The Maxwell children—a huddle of cheeping, underfed sparrows—came in for their daily supply of liquorice allsorts. When they had gone, she said, "You'll be late at Major Driver's, Jim. See that they give you some tea with your lunch. It's a bit windy."

She felt ashamed of her solicitude for his health, remembering how hostile scandal had said that she only married him for his physical strength; and now it was her 'wiry' strength which never failed. But this time he countered her sympathy. "I don't like you not sleeping," he said, "you must speak to Doctor about it. They can give you something for that nowadays."

"What do you know about my sleeping," she cried with mocking indignation, "snoring your head off." She was overcome with tenderness for him and resented it. What could the underlying tenderness do to mend the broken surface of their daily life together? "Besides it's early closing, thank heaven," she said brightly, "I'm going to tea with Eileen Carter."

"Ah! that'll do you good," he said, smiling, showing the perfect, even white teeth she still delighted to see. She knew, however, how little he liked her friendship with Eileen—that ladylike companion of books and gardening and religion in which he had no part.

Miss Meadows came in for some elastic, but Jim disregarded her presence. He went up to Esther and whispered, "It'd be far better to let the old woman go as the doctor wants."

Esther only shook her head in reply. She had brought him no children to care for, she was not going to let his mother be taken away. She turned away from him towards Miss Meadows, but as she passed him, he pressed the back of his hand against hers and whispered, "Thank you, my old Esther." It was a gesture and words he had not used for so long, a gesture which recalled intensely the days of their clandestine love-making, their occasional secret pressures and touches when they met in shop or market square, wherever there were people who made open recognition impossible in the days before the scandal broke. The tenderness that filled her this time was so little touched by irritation, that Miss Meadows, receiving her card of elastic, said, "The cold weather agrees with you all right, Mrs Barrington, but there, you're always on the move."

Perhaps the re-awakened and unalloyed tenderness for Jim would have died beneath the anæsthetic of the day's tedious chores had not a chance customer revived the past in Esther's feelings. For all those years in the remoteness of their Yorkshire farm, she had dreaded an utterly improbable chance contact with neighbours from Sussex who would revive the years of scandal, who even at worst might break down the wall which she had built around Jim's wounded self-esteem. But in these last years, with her father dead, and her mother gone to join Rosamund in Kenya, the Sussex faces had faded out in dimness, the thought of their intrusion had ceased to fret her. Yet here, of course, in the shop, remote though their Midland village was from the South, the chance was far greater and on that very morning it turned to certainty.

The face of the man who entered the shop was familiar, the voice that asked for cigarettes made her sure. It was Charles Stanton still bearing traces of the fourteen-year-old boy who, round-eyed, had once stared at her so fascinatedly as the subject of mysterious adult whispering. Childhood visual memory was apparently less enduring, for he left the shop without recognising her. She peered through the stacked boxes of Puffed Wheat and tins of cocoa in the window. There indeed in the Ford Consul sat Mrs Stanton, motherly, vulgar, overdressed, hardly changed indeed from the woman who, with more titillated curiosity than her small son's, had befriended her in those isolated days after the scandal broke. For a moment memory of the old woman's kindness made Esther start

for the door to hail the passing tourists; then a sharp
recollection of how difficult even kindness had been to
endure forced her back into the shop's safety. With relief
she heard the car drive off; but that momentary impulse of
Charles Stanton to stop for cigarettes, Mrs Stanton's love
for touring with her son, had broken through the blanket-
ing mist that weariness had interposed between Esther
and the "worst fortnight of her life".

If she had her way, indeed if her mother's will had prevailed, she would not have stayed one day at the vicarage
after Jim's wife had made her scene. But her father had
been so determined. "If you care for me at all, Esther,
you will stay and fight it out. I will try to help you, even
to forgive you, as long as you do not run away. I can
forgive anything—indeed I should hardly be a minister
of Christ if I could not—but cowards I will not forgive."
It had been nothing to do with her, of course; it was part
of his relentless fight against his parishioners. "I will
teach these people Christ's charity even if I can do so only
with the rod of shame." Of course, he could not and at
the end of a fortnight, he had been relieved when she
ended his fight for him by running away.

Why indeed should the parish have forgiven her? She
had betrayed her class, her Church and her sex. They had
not shared the passion which had sustained and driven
her. If she had been outside that passion, she would have
been on their side. Only Mrs Stanton—"My dear, you're
always welcome here I'm sure. Not that that'll help you
with the county, I'm afraid. You know what they think
of Henry and me. Rich trade that's us. But who cares
what they say? They think the days of carriage folk are

still with us, stupid creatures." And then her sentimental
curiosity—"Well, love certainly suits her, doesn't it,
Henry? I never seen you in such good features, my dear."
Old Mr Stanton, too, just a little more familiar than he
should have been. Esther had hated herself for needing
their support and hated herself, too, for disliking it; but
she could not bear their coating her passion with their
sticky sentimentalism—"You must always follow your
heart in life, my dear." She had longed to reject Mrs
Stanton as Marianne had rejected Mrs Jennings, but then
Marianne had not committed adultery with her Wil-
loughby.

Little by little the memories faded from her mind at the
chivvying and poking, the day's demands—the accounts,
the customers' gossip, the orders, the telephone. She was
left, as she closed the shop at one o'clock only with an
overwhelming tenderness for Jim.

As tea-time approached Eileen Carter became as excited
as a schoolgirl. Although a strict guardian of her conscience, she was not inclined to be conscious of her own
moods—to have been so would have seemed to her
dangerously near to emotional fudge Her present elation,
however, was too violent to escape her notice and she
told herself sharply not to be swoony. Esther Barrington
was a good, brave little woman; it was lucky for both of
them that they had broken through the barriers of shyness, for loneliness helped nobody in this world; she was
only so pleased that her comfortable sufficiency in life
allowed her to brighten a little the drudge-like existence

of someone so decent; that was all there was to it All the
rest *was* fudge.

As she passed through the kitchen to the garden, old
Madge glowed warmth at her. "I'm making some of
those griddle cakes Mrs Barrington loves. It does one
good to see her enjoying herself, doesn't it, Miss Eileen."
Eileen's usual gruff notes were almost a bark as she
answered, "All right, Madge, but don't worry me with
it I'm up to my eyes in work" And so she was, she
thought, with twenty herbaceous plants to move; the
work ought to have been done a week ago.

It was, therefore, a vast prospect of buttocks stretching
tight a chocolate and white striped cloth skirt that con-
fronted Esther as she turned into the garden at a quarter
to four that afternoon.

"Heavens above! Eileen," she cried, "surely you're
not putting *more* plants into that border."

Eileen's pink cheeks were scarlet almost to apoplexy
point as she swung her broad shoulders round to face her
visitor.

"I'm only moving these damned phloxes," she grunted,
"every one's got a hell of a great root. God knows
whether they're worth moving, they're probably riddled
with bloody eelworm." It was a mark of her shyness that
she used to Eileen the 'bad language' that she normally
only employed in her voluntary social work to show that
she was not an old frump.

"But surely you can tell."

"No, I *can't*," Eileen said emphatically, "the damned
leaves are all floppy but that may be due to this summer's
drought."

"You should let Jim come and advise you," Esther said. In her present mood, she rushed to get in her husband's name as soon as possible.

Eileen Carter ran her hand through her untidy greying black bob with impatience. "I have some pretentions to being a gardener myself, Esther," she said.

"A very good one," her friend replied, "but Jim poor dear has to know these things professionally."

"Professional gardeners in my experiences," Eileen said, "always make a balls up."

Esther's pretty blue eyes flashed angrily for a moment in her thinned lined face, then she decided that the poor old thing was in one of her moods. "Most of them do, of course," she said. "Double begonias and calceolarias, they couldn't have more ghastly taste." Her voice, as she spoke, took on the upper-middle class drawl she had only found again recently in her friendship with Eileen.

They talked for a while about gardening and, as they talked, Eileen lost her shy coarseness and Esther slipped more completely into drawling assurance.

"Well," Eileen asked, as they sat over china tea, griddle cakes and home-made quince cheese, "and how is the Mum, dotty as ever?" She habitually referred to the mothers she visited in her family welfare work as "the mums", it was a mark of her attitude to Jim that she called old Mrs Barrington by this name.

"Oh dear!" Esther said, "poor old thing, her memory gets worse every day. She was such a good, kind person, Eileen, even if she was always a very simple soul. I can't bear to see her in this childish state. I gave her sardines for breakfast and nothing would stop her dipping them in her tea."

Eileen threw back her bulldog head and wheezed with laughter. For a moment Esther was on the point of joining in, when she remembered Jim. "It isn't a laughing matter, Eileen," she said. Her handkerchief was rolled into a ball in the palm of her hand; she dug nails her into it with anger at betraying Jim—she should never have spoken of Mother's pathetic childishness.

Eileen looked at her unperturbed. "Oh yes it is, my dear," she said, "sickness, death, even sin, all have their absurdities. And God intended that we should laugh at them. As long as it's not cruel laughter." She lit one of her small cheroots—her only capitulation to eccentricity. "Jane understood it well enough as you know. She could laugh at Mrs Musgrave's fat tears over her scapegoat son, but Emma's cruel jibe at Miss Bates could not be forgiven. It's as simple as that or, rather, like everything else in life, as difficult." When she spoke her ethical convictions, her gruff voice became almost absurdly offhand and flat.

Esther took a last piece of currant bread to finish her quince cheese. "Jane Austen was awfully clever," she said, "but even when I'm enjoying her books most, I sometimes wonder whether she ever knew what it was like to be laughed at."

"What?" Eileen questioned. "A surplus old maid?" Then embarrassed by this degree of self-revelation, she added, "The trouble with you, my dear, is that you're a Jane Bennett and not an Eliza. You take too good a view of the world. You let it trample on you."

"Oh!" cried Esther, "I have had enough of revolt to last me for my life. I don't ever want to fight people again, I just want to be left alone to get on with my work and God knows there's enough of it." Then she looked across at Eileen's glowing fire, the samplers, the bellows, the etchings of Lichfield Cathedral. "What I'd most like in all the world," she said, stretching her thin body with an easiness unusual for her neat, trim manner, "would be some comfort, some ease of living like this. Or rather," she added earnestly, "I should like it for Jim."

Eileen's heavy face seemed to lose all life, to become a smooth, fleshy mass. "I can't quite see dear old Jim at Throckings," she said with a chuckle that was not some-how warm.

Esther still stretched relaxed. "Can't you?" She spoke from far away. "You don't know Jim at all, do you, Eileen?"

"He's not very easy to know," Eileen answered stiffly.

"Isn't that the best kind?" Esther asked, then as though she had returned to the room again suddenly, she said in a light gay voice, "Oh! Eileen, you can't think how much it means to be able to come and relax here. You *are* a dear person, you know."

Eileen's heavy head bent down for a moment in girlish shyness. "I wish you would come far more often," she said.

"Oh! my dear, if I could . . ." Esther laughed. "But how could I? Who's to give Jim his tea?"

Eileen got up and stood for a moment by her chair, her thick legs ungainly set apart. "Thou shalt not make unto thyself any graven image," she said. She moved across the room and fingered the dried hydrangeas on the window-table. "It's awful here on rainy days," she said absently. Then coming behind Esther she placed a square hand on her shoulder and pressed it. The gesture of intimacy was familiar to her friend. "You're worth such a lot more than you think," Eileen said, then she stroked Esther's greying fair hair. It was a gesture entirely unfamiliar to her friend and she got up hurriedly pushing Eileen's hand to one side. She went over to the mirror above the fireplace and patted her hair into place. Eileen sat down on the sofa, legs apart, heavy bosom forward, squat and lowering.

Esther stared into the mirror and spoke without turning round. "I suppose I've lost the art of friendship," she said. "You've no idea what's it like to be a lawbreaker in decent society. And that's what Jim and I were. We broke every rule in the book. I pray for forgiveness and God, I trust will forgive me. But the world—especially the village world—isn't God."

Eileen laughed, "Oh, you make it sound like one of those novels I used to read as a girl. By Sheila Kaye-Smith or someone like that. Fifteen years ago in Sussex! My dear, times have changed."

"Oh, I know," Esther still did not look at her friend, "but the county haven't. About adultery, perhaps, but they don't forgive anyone who oversteps their precious class barrier."

"You live in the past," Eileen declared. A gleam appeared in her usually dulled eyes, "Besides even if you're right, it isn't as noticeable as all that. You've acquired a good deal of protective colouring through the years, you know."

Esther swung round; for a moment her soft blue eyes showed horror.

"Oh, my dear!" Eileen boomed, "I've said the wrong thing. If that's what worries you, put your mind at rest. 'Once a lady' as our mums used to say. For what it's worth."

After the Show

ALL the way home in the taxi and in the lift up to her flat on the seventh floor Mrs Liebig kept on talking. Sometimes she spoke of the play, making comments to Maurice in the form of questions to which she did not await the answer. The lights of Regent Street and Oxford Street flashed momentarily through the taxi window, caught in the saxe-blue spangles of the ornament that crowned her almost saxe-blue neatly waved hair, reflected in the mirror of her powder compact which seemed always to occupy her attention in taxis. "Was the father of the girl a fraud then?" she asked, and, "Why didn't the mother make him work?" "I suppose," she said, "that the old man had used him to get rid of his mistress." Then, "What a play," she exclaimed, "for a boy of your age to take his grandmother to! But it's clever, of course, too clever, I think. There weren't any real animals you know, in the cage. That was clever."

More often she commented on family affairs. "Your father needs a real rest," she said, "let's hope your mother sees that he gets it. It's not the way to take holidays—mixing business up with pleasure. Of course your mother will want to spend a lot of time with her own people, that's only natural. They have a very nice house, you know, the Engelmanns in Cologne. Or they used to have. Anything might have happened to it now. But she *must* think of your father all the same. That won't be much of a holiday for Norman, talking German all the time. Though he's a wonderful linguist, your father, you know."

Once she said, "Well we must try to imagine what they are doing now," but the effort was apparently too great for her, because she went straight on, "Lending her house to those Parkinsons. What a thing for your mother to do! But then they don't have to think about money, so there'd be no sense in all the trouble of letting." Her tone was at once reverent and sarcastic.

Maurice said nothing, indeed he hardly stirred, except once or twice to light Mrs Liebig's cigarette with the lighter she handed him from her bag. She shared his parents' constant concern that he should have perfect manners with women. After the theatre, his slim body, usually so loosely and naturally elegant, remained tense— a tailors' dummy woodenness perhaps more in keeping with the slightly overcareful elegance of his clothes than his usual poise. A tension too came into the expression of his large dark eyes, ordinarily a trifle cow-like in their placid, liquid sensuality. It was not so much that he remained hypnotically bewitched by the play's deception, but rather that he dreaded returning from its dramatic reality to the fraudulent flatness of his own life. He seemed to strain every nerve to keep the play in action, to spin out at least its mood from the theatre into the commonplace texture of his own life. His apprehension announced his experience that the task was vain, his nervous elation a certain fear that he might on this occasion succeed. It was the same, too, with every theatrical performance from Shakespeare to musical comedy. In addition to this adolescent histrionic restlessness, however, there was a somewhat plodding seriousness which demanded a peculiarly strong response to 'good' plays.

To-night, after *The Wild Duck*, then, his earnest good taste reinforced his emotions in their struggle against the invasion of his grandmother's voice. The underlying Jewish cockney note of her cracked contralto jarred more than usual and he could not condemn his unfeeling snobbery without also condemning his mother, for Mrs Norman Liebig was forever saying that "grandmother's voice was such a pity."

As they entered the hall of the flat, old Mrs Liebig's well corsetted plump body collided as usual against one of the giant size Japanese pots as she searched for the light switch, but she still continued to talk. "Well, there it is," she said, "so the poor little girl committed suicide. No wonder with a father who was a liar and did nothing all day. All the same," she said, and the electric light shone brightly upon heavily rouged high cheekbones, "I don't think a little girl like that would shoot herself. More likely the mother—tied to such a man."

Maurice took her black moiré silk evening coat off her shoulders, and folded it carefully, smoothing the squirrel-skin collar; then he said, "Gregers Werle was a fanatic. In his false determination to expose the truth, he destroyed the poetry in Hedwig's life and drove her to her death."

His voice was a shade higher than usual and its normal slight sibilance had a hissing edge. Even Mrs Liebig was struck by the fierceness of his tone, she looked up for a moment from the telephone pad on which the maid had noted a message. "Oh, it's a dreadful thing all right," she said, "to destroy young people's dreams." But there was a limit to her sentiment, or perhaps she remembered her own comfortable, prosaic childhood, for she added, "What a way to bring a child up! With all those fancies. No," she said emphatically, "it's not the sort of thing I'd have gone to if you hadn't taken me. But I'm glad I've seen it. The acting was fine."

In the sitting-room the brown velvet sofa and easy chairs looked hot and uninviting on this warm spring evening. Mrs Liebig automatically moved one or two of the daffodils in the thick shell-shaped white earthenware vase. She crossed the room and drew the long heavy velvet curtains, shutting out the night breeze. "Go on, Maurice," she said, "help yourself, tuck in." And she slapped the handle of the silver-shaded green metal cocktail wagon. "Your father said you could have two beers or one whisky."

Maurice gave himself a lager and turned to his grandmother, but she answered his gesture before he spoke, "No, I'll have my nightcap after my bath," she said, but she helped herself to a large canapé of prawns in aspic from a white-and-gold-painted metal table. "Go on," she said again, "tuck in."

Maurice surveyed the array of gelatinous hors d'œuvres. The Norman Liebigs also always had a mass of foodstuff awaiting their return from the theatre, but true to her

German origin, Mrs Norman saw that everything was cooked at home. Maurice could hear his mother's disapproving tones—"Poor Grandmother lives from Selfridge's cooked provision counter"—so he contented himself with a cheese straw.

Mrs Liebig trotted out of the room and came back with the rubber ice container from the refrigerator. She dropped a square of ice with the tongs into Maurice's beer and kissed his forehead. She was happy to have for a while a man to wait on. "So there you are, my dear," she said. "That was your Uncle Victor phoned while we were out. Ah, well, some trouble again. Money for the dogs or for that Sylvia. It comes to the same thing, my dear. In any case it can wait for to-morrow."

At the mention of his Uncle Victor's name, Maurice's curved nostril dilated for a moment, adding to the camel-like arrogance of his thin, sensitive face. Mrs Liebig flushed above her rouged cheekbones to her temples.

"Oh, there's no good putting your head in the air at your Uncle's name, my dear. He hasn't had your father's luck nor his brain. But business brains aren't everything. I know. I've got them. I've made money, but that's not all in life." Her grandson's complete stillness seemed to anger her, for she added loudly, "Who built your father's business up, eh? And they can't do anything now, you know, my dear, unless *I* agree. I'm still a director. What does your mother say to that?"

To this attack on his mother, Maurice answered quietly, "We see Aunt Paula regularly."

It had all the effect he desired. Mrs Liebig's large dark eyes narrowed with fury. "All right, you see your Aunt

Paula. So do I. And she's a clever buyer and she knows it. But that's not flesh and blood. What if your Uncle Victor did leave her? How did she treat him? I can't understand your father. He knows the world. He knows well enough that Paula only married Victor because she thought he would be a success. And when he wasn't, she turned to and made success for herself. All right, she's a clever girl. But all the time she let him know it. That's not love."

"Father helped Uncle Victor for years," Maurice said coldly. He took out an orange-wood stick and began to clean his nails.

"And you've got clean nails and he hasn't," Mrs Liebig cried. "Very good. Yes, your father helped Victor. So did I. So should we all, his family. Rose sends him money from New York. It's flesh and blood, my dear. I could hardly *tell* Rose that your father doesn't see Victor any more. She asked me how the hell can they be like that when they're brothers. And now *you're* not to see Victor. Your mother told me, 'We don't wish Maurice to meet Victor.' She wants to have it every way. The Liebigs are no good because they have no culture. 'Norman doesn't care for music. I want Maurice to care for things besides money.' Very well. Your Uncle Victor cares for things besides money and he's a Liebig. He's a good artist. His cartoons made money and then those film people changed their minds and so he didn't make any more money. Oh, yes, your mother likes artists, but she doesn't like them to be out of work. I know."

Maurice rose and picked up a book from the table. "I

can't listen to you if you talk about Mother like this," he said.

"What do you mean you can't listen? A boy of your age," Mrs Liebig cried. "You'll listen to what I choose to tell you, my dear. You're going to Cambridge and you're going to be a lawyer. Nothing to do with the rag business for Gertrude Liebig's son. Well, designing dresses and selling them has more art in it than arguing in law courts. You listen to sense for once instead of to your 'Wild Ducks'. Mustn't meet your own uncle. You're old enough to decide for yourself."

She was breathless by now with anger and sweating through her heavy make-up. She put her hand to her breast. "That's the sort of fool I am, upsetting myself for a foolish boy. All this has nothing to do with you," she shouted, "discussing your uncle at your age. Why, you're only just seventeen." She drew her compact, plump little body to its full five feet four. "I'm going to have my bath," she said and walked trimly out of the room, teetering a little as always in her very high heels.

Maurice arranged himself negligently on the striped period Regency couch in order to control his rising hysteria. Because these people, his father, his mother, his grandmother had conditioned him to love them, they had no scruple in tearing him apart. "Very well," as his grandmother said, they had him emotionally, but his mind remained entirely indifferent, even contemptuous—no, not contemptuous, for that involved some engagement—to them. He chose carefully the words in which he set his thoughts—'emotionally', 'involved', 'engagement'—for words shaped one's thinking. He could forgive them working off their loneliness, their ambitions, their nervous exhaustion on him; what he could not forgive—or rather accept, for forgiveness suggested some demand on his part and he asked nothing of them—what he could not *accept* was this inclusion in their empty, flat lives. Yes, even his mother, with her cultural aspirations; it was almost easier for someone with ideas to accept a woman like his grandmother with her tough, vulgar pushing ways.

Carefully adjusting the sharp creases of his chocolate-brown trousers as he crossed his legs, he applied himself to Burke's speeches. Through the clever passion and the stirring elegance of the oratory he tried to control his impatience, his furious wish to have the years pass more quickly so that he could live a proper life of high responsibility, of tempered adult courage. For this age of mediocrity, of grubbing merchants and sordid artisans—this age of Liebigs would pass; he and his generation would see to that. But meanwhile, if only something would happen—something real and not just on the stage.

When Mrs Liebig emerged from the bathroom, she poked her head round the sitting-room door. Between the folds of her gold thread dressing-gown, her breasts showed sagging; her face was flat, dead with vanishing cream; her blued hair frizzed out from a silver hair-net. "How's your book, Maurice?" she asked with a smile. Anger was soon gone with her. "We must get the man to the T.V., my dear. It's not right for it to go wrong like this. I paid a lot of money for that machine. Get me my night-cap," she said, "I'll be back in a minute. On the rocks," she added. She had brought the phrase back from her visit to her daughter Rose in New York and she loved to use it.

When she returned to her strong whisky, she settled down to her favourite half an hour's chat before bed. She had the impression that the daily routine of her life left no time for real conversation, although she had never been silent even at the height of her active career as Madame Clara, modiste.

She tried this evening to keep her talk off family matters. "I don't know what I shall do next winter," she said. "The Palace is closing down. There's not another hotel like it in Madeira. They've known me since before your grandfather died. The head porter always asks after you—the young gentleman with the books."

As Maurice made no answer, she tried hard to connect with him. "The boys still dive, you know," she said. "Crabs and sponges." The words in her mouth brought Maurice no evocation of sub-tropical romance. "I wonder if Senhora Paloes will be at Biarritz this year. She plays very high stakes. These Brazilians are so rich, you know, my dear." But her annual holidays—Madeira in February, Biarritz in June—were so much a routine even to her, that she could find little to say of them.

"Well," she asked, "who are you meeting to-morrow? The Clarkson girl or Betty Lewis?"

"I'm going out with some friends from school," Maurice said firmly to avoid his grandmother's roguish innuendo, but to no avail.

"You prefer the little blondes, don't you, Maurice? She was very pretty, that girl in the stalls."

Despite his annoyance at her noticing his glances in the

theatre, he did not wish to appear priggish, so he said, "Yes, wasn't she?"

"That's what I tell your mother," Mrs Liebig said. "Let Maurice find his girls for himself. Always arranging theatre parties for the Clarksons or dinner dances with Adela Siegl's girl. He'll go out with his old grandmother when he's with *me*, I said. Let him find his girls for himself."

Maurice did not wish to side too openly with her against his mother, so he merely smiled.

"And to-morrow evening a nice show for *me*," Mrs Liebig continued, "a nice musical show—*The Pajama Game*. Rose saw it in New York. She said it was tops. Not a show for *you* this time. A show for the children. For the old girl." She laughed in delight at her little joke —a harsh braying jay sound that seemed almost to call forth an answering note from the telephone.

"Oh, my dear, so late," Mrs Liebig exclaimed. "You answer, Maurice. Is it Victor? What does he want? I can't speak now. It's too late." She chattered on, so that Maurice had to stop one ear with a finger to hear his correspondent.

"You're wanted at once," he said. "Sylvia is very ill. Uncle Victor's not there. They can't find him."

"Well, I can't go like this," Mrs Liebig was indignant. "What's she got? A pain or something?"

"It's very urgent," Maurice said, speaking gravely as though the person at the other side might hear Mrs Liebig's levity. "She's had an accident."

"Oh, my God!" Mrs Liebig cried. "The damned fool girl. Poor Victor! Well, what can I do?"

"Mrs Liebig will come as soon as possible. I shall come immediately," Maurice said into the telephone. "I'm Mrs Victor Liebig's nephew."

Mrs Liebig got up from her chair, drawing the gold and green dressing-gown round her, slopping a little in her mules. "You can't go *there*," she said. "What do you mean 'Mrs Victor Liebig's nephew'? You've never seen the girl?"

Maurice said, "Someone must go. The woman on the phone wouldn't say exactly, but she implied that it wasn't an accident. I think she wanted to say that Sylvia had tried to kill herself." His eyes were no longer flat and dead. "She couldn't find anyone else," he said, as though that clinched the matter.

But for his grandmother it did not. "Oh, my God!" she cried. "What does Victor want to mix up with such little fools for? I should never have agreed to meet the girl," she added, as though her recognition of her son's mistress had given the girl aspirations above her station, encouraged her to ideas of suicide.

Maurice seemed not to hear her. "You'd better get dressed as soon as you can and follow me over there," he said and moved to the door. Mrs Liebig ran after him, holding her dressing-gown round her with one hand, she put the other on his arm. "I don't know what . . ." she said. "Norman will never forgive me. You'll have to answer to your mother, you know. You're not to meet Victor and now you rush off to see his girl. I don't know . . ." Maurice went out of the room. She followed him, shouting into the darkness of the hall. "They're not married, you know." She knew perfectly well that he knew, she shouted it as though it were a threat. Only the click of the front door latch answered her.

At first, in the taxi, sailing down an empty Baker Street, Maurice was only aware that monotony had been broken; held up by lights at the Edgware Road junction, however, he became nervous of what he would find at the end of his journey. The urgent and mysterious voice on the telephone had enveloped him at once in drama; he couldn't at that moment have handed over his part to his grandmother, however little he knew his lines. Now, however, apprehension made him search for evasions: if the Liebigs were in the caste, he thought, even courtesy Liebigs like Sylvia, it was bound to turn out to be some sordid melodrama. With the taxi in progress again, he felt the elation of duty; if the cause he was serving had neither quite the glory nor the high intent that he would have liked, at least there was a cause to serve—and this, as all his little group knew well, was what their generation had been cheated of. Besides how few of his friends were likely to be involved with mistresses who tried to commit suicide, he reflected with a glow of pride.

Pride, however, has its fall, and as the taxi-driver braked sharply to avoid a drunk at Westbourne Grove, Maurice was jolted into disgust at his childishness. He blushed with shame as though one of his friends— Gervase or Selwyn Adcock—had heard his thoughts. They were all agreed, of course, the whole group, that sin to-day was as drab and inglorious as virtue. "Simply the blowsy Brittania on the reverse of the fake coin," Gervase had said last term. By the time the taxi drew up at 42, Branksombe Terrace, Maurice had found many reasons to support his anxious dislike of his self-imposed chivalry.

As he looked out at the dirty mid-Victorian house with its peeling stucco and straggles of grimy Virginia creeper, he saw a world whose unfamiliarity daunted him. He longed for the central heating, the books, the modern reading lamp, the iced drink, of his bedroom in his grand-mother's flat. There were theatres too cheap and squalid to play in. Maurice was about to tear up his contract and tell the taxi-driver to take him home, when the front door opened and a thin, dark-haired young woman in blue jeans came out on to the steps. "Mr Liebig," she called, in an over-refined, slightly petulant voice. "Mr Liebig? This is the house." Maurice got out and paid the fare.

"I'm Freda Cherrill," the young woman said. "The person who phoned to you." Her thin, yellowish face looked so drawn and tired, and her voice was so languid that Maurice felt that he dared not question her. She drew him into a little ill-lit hall and bent her long neck— yellow and grubby above her blue and white striped shirt —down towards him. Her large dark eyes were vacant rather than sad. Her breath came scented but a little sour as she whispered into his face. "I'd better give you all the gen before you go in," she said, and pointing towards the door at their side. "She's in there."

Maurice felt able to assert himself. "Is the doctor with her?" he asked.

"I'm afraid not," Miss Cherrill replied a little petulantly. "He was dining in Putney, but he's on his way."

"But surely," Maurice cried, "there was some doctor nearer."

"I only know Dr Waters," Miss Cherrill replied. "She doesn't seem to have a doctor of her own." Her languid voice became quite sharp with disapproval. "So naturally I had to send for mine. He's always been very good with my anæmia and he's a very understanding man."

"I don't know what has happened," Maurice said, cutting through her petulance with a certain hauteur.

"Well, I couldn't very well say everything on the phone, could I?" Miss Cherrill was quite annoyed. "She doesn't want Mr Morello and everybody else involved."

"Where is my uncle?" Maurice asked.

"Oh!" Miss Cherrill said scornfully, "if we knew that. . . . She's comfortable enough now. I kept walking her up and down the room at first, I thought I had to keep her awake, she was so dozey, but Dr Walters said she hadn't taken enough to make it serious and in any case with aspirins . . ."

"So she *has* tried to commit suicide."

"I told you so," Miss Cherrill said angrily.

"I didn't quite understand."

"Well, you can see the telephone's in the hall. She asked me not to bring everybody into it. Morello's room's only down there." She pointed along the hall. "I don't know them," she spoke quite loudly in her annoyance. "I heard her crying. My room's next door. It went on for ages so I went in."

"You've been very good," Maurice said. "Thank you."

"It was lucky I was washing my hair," Miss Cherrill replied—"I nearly always go out of a Wednesday. Besides, it's not often anything happens in life, is it?"

Maurice felt disgusted by his own emotions expressed

from another mouth, so he said, "I think I'd better go in and see her."

"Of course," Miss Cherrill said, "someone ought to be very stern with her. I told her myself that it could have meant a police case, and would do now if I hadn't had a word with Dr Waters. Not that he probably won't be pretty sharp with her himself, I expect. She's *got* to be frightened." All Miss Cherrill's sympathy, even her pleasure at events out of the ordinary were dissipating now that someone else was taking over: she was very tired, she was going out the next evening and her hair was still filthy. "Well," she said in final tones, "I'm glad there's somebody else here she knows at last. She's still very weepy and a bit dazed. She's been awfully sick, you know."

"I'm afraid," said Maurice, "that she doesn't know me at all. We've never met." Miss Cherrill stared at him in disgust.

"Well," she said, "I suppose it's all right. You're very young, aren't you? But it's only someone to sit with her. And, anyway, she doesn't seem to have any real people." She opened Sylvia's door and peered in. "She's all right for you to come in," she said, and then, her refined petulance leaving her for a moment. "The smell of sick isn't too bad, is it? I've drenched the room in eau-de-Cologne." She whispered loudly and with relish. Maurice said nothing; even the faintest smell of vomit made his stomach heave in protest.

Apart from the double bed in the corner and one broken-down, hair-oil-stained armchair, the room seemed as bare as it was large. The only dressing-table was made from something that looked like an inverted packing-case. On it were crowded lotions, creams and powders; above it hung some home-made contraption that had brought the electricity by means of a profusion of wires from its lonely eminence in the centre of the high ceiling. The walls were cream-distempered and dirty; someone had started to cover one of them with a cheap 'modernistic' wallpaper. Over an old towel-horse hung a black skirt, a white muslin blouse, stockings and underwear. There were books and magazines in scattered heaps on the matting-covered floor; an uncovered typewriter crowded, with a portable gramophone and records, the small top of a rickety varnished bedside table. On the walls were pinned, in profuse disorder, Victor's drawings, giving the room the appearance of a school art exhibition. In the bed Sylvia lay. Against the blue whiteness of her face the bed linen showed grey, and the pillow-case shone greasy under her thick but dirty fair hair.

Despite all the pallor and the grubbiness, however, she looked so young and delicious to Maurice—especially so much younger than he had expected, no older perhaps than he was—that he was unable to speak and he felt the giddiness and trembling of the legs which lust always brought to his repressed body. Her eyes seemed to him extraordinarily sensual under their drowsing, half closed, red lids; her white cheeks were nevertheless plump about their high pommets and her heavy lips were half opened in a Greuze-like pout. She looked altogether like some eighteenth-century print of a young dying harlot—ostensibly a morality, in fact a bait for prurient eyes.

Maurice felt embarrassedly that Miss Cherrill's eyes

were upon him, putting his manhood to the test. He
summoned all his wits to find something to say—something that would mark his authority. Before he could find
words, however, Sylvia's sobbing swelled to convulsive
breathing and then burst into a loud, hysterical weeping—
the hideous, uncontrolled crying of a frightened, spoilt
child. With children Maurice knew himself to be
powerless.

Miss Cherrill looked at him for a moment, then she
walked over and shook Sylvia roughly. "Stop that noise
at once," she said. "You'll look a fool if the doctor finds
you like this." Her action had no effect except that Sylvia
hit out at her flat bosom.

"Go away," she cried. "Go away all of you. I won't see
you or your bloody doctor."

It seemed to Maurice that if he could do nothing with
Sylvia, he could at least order Miss Cherrill about. "I
think you'd better leave us," he said.

"I'm sure I've no wish to stay," Miss Cherrill replied.
"This has been a lesson to me, I can tell you."

Maurice opened the door for her, "Thank you very
much for all you have done," he said, but she went out
without looking at him.

He stood for a moment staring at Sylvia. He was
embarrassed at the pleasure her crying brought to him.
It was not, however, his first intimation of the quirks of
sexual desire. He hastened to efface the disturbing
emotion with redoubled kindness. "I should like very
much to help you if I can." The words when they came
seemed very inadequate and stiffly formal; their effect on
Sylvia however, was immediate.

I

"Get out of here, get out of here," she screamed. "I want to be left alone."

The request seemed to Maurice so reasonable that he was about to walk out, when Sylvia leaned over the side of the bed and, picking up a slipper from the floor, she threw it at his head. Her half-doped aim was feebly wide of the mark. Nevertheless, it produced a strange effect on Maurice; he walked very deliberately over to the bed and smacked Sylvia's face. Then he kissed her clumsily and excitedly on the mouth. Her breath, sour through the eau-de-Cologne fumes, checked his excitement. The whole chain of his behaviour was so surprising to him that he just sat on the bed and stared not at Sylvia but slightly over her head.

"You look like a fish," she said. She was not crying now, but he realised that her ordinary speaking voice was strangely husky.

"I'm sorry," he said, "I came here to help you."

"You do," she said.

To Maurice her strangely direct but slightly goofy manner recalled so much that he had heard in the theatre. If he had met neither the tragedy nor even the melodrama for which he had been prepared, here surely at least was English comedy at its best. He tried to forget the appearance of the room. Decor was after all an over-rated aspect of the stage. He, too, must be laconic, off hand, bohemian, modern.

"Why did you do it?" he asked.

The question, alas, only brought on crying so violent that he could hardly hear himself speak. "You'll only bring Miss Cherrill back," he shouted.

"She's an interfering cow," Sylvia sobbed. "I hate her."

"She's been very kind, I should have thought."

"She wasn't, she just wanted to gloat."

"Oh! please," Maurice cried, "don't let's discuss that. Can't you tell me what's wrong?"

"Why should I?" Sylvia asked, "I don't know you."

This, however, seemed unreasonable, so Maurice said, "Why did you get Miss Cherrill to ring up my grandmother if you didn't want our help?"

This again set Sylvia crying. "You think I didn't mean to do it. You think I got frightened. That's what you'll tell Victor, isn't it? It's easy to say someone is just a hysteric." And when he made no answer, "Go on, that's what you think, isn't it?" she cried.

It was, in fact, what Maurice was thinking, as far as he could in her presence; but as he had had no experience of hysterics, he did not feel fully justified in making the judgment; and, in any case, if she was, it was surely most important to calm her, since both shaking and slapping which he had always supposed to be the sovereign remedies had failed. "I think you must be very unhappy," he said, "and if I can help you I should like to do so." It was not perhaps the high purpose in life which his generation was seeking, but it was a sincere wish.

It did, indeed, also succeed in calming Sylvia a little. "I'm in such a mess," she said, "such a terrible mess. I've let myself love a man who's a liar, a real hopeless liar. And that's a terrible thing to do!" She announced this gravely as one of the profound, the ultimate truths of life. "He says there isn't someone else," she said, "but I know better. I know her name. It's Hilda. Isn't it awful?" She began once more to sob.

Maurice could not feel this so deeply, but he said, "It's not a very nice name certainly."

Sylvia immediately began to pound on his leg with her small clenched fists. "Oh, you silly little fool," she shouted, "Victor's left me. Can't you understand? He's left me. All Thursday I guessed he was going and I said to him, 'Victor, if you don't love me any more, well then tell me. I can take it,' I said. But he just smiled, smiled to madden me. 'You want me to get mad at you,' I said, 'so that you can have your excuse. Well, I'm not going to do it. I can take the truth,' I told him. Well," she cried, turning suddenly on Maurice, "if I am hard and tough before I should be, what made me that way? What's life done for little Sylvia Wright?"

If she had intended an answer to this vital question, Maurice was not to hear it, for at that moment there was a noise of braking outside the house, of voices raised, of bells rung. Among the voices Maurice could hear his grandmother's. He moved to the door, wishing that he could kiss Sylvia again before Mrs Liebig came on the scene.

"You can't even bother to listen to me and yet you ask me how it happened. I think you are despicable," Sylvia said.

It was true that he had ceased listening to her as soon as a rival noise came to attract his attention, but then her torrent of words had been so sudden and so uncontrolled.

"You think because I've been in prison . . ."

"I knew nothing about that," Maurice interrupted.

"But in any case I can't let my grandmother stand out there for ever."

When he came into the hall, a little old woman in a dressing-gown was making her way crabwise and very slowly down the stairs. "Everyone's in such a hurry nowadays," she said, "I'm coming as quickly as I can."

"I think they're ringing for me," Maurice said.

"Well, I didn't suppose they were ringing for *me*," the old woman replied, but she began slowly and with heavy dragging of her feet to go back up the stairs.

Before Maurice could get to the front door, however, another door at the end of the passage opened and a plump, dark young man, also in a dressing-gown, stuck his head out. "If that ringing's for you," he said, "I should be obliged if you'd answer it quickly." Before Maurice could answer, he added, "If you're connected with Mrs Liebig I may as well tell you now that I have the whole matter under review." The door closed again and he was gone.

When Maurice opened the front door, he found a clean-shaven, middle-aged man in evening dress standing on the step. He was smoking a pipe and looked, Maurice thought, like a naval officer. There was no sign of Mrs Liebig.

"Liebig?" asked the man shortly. It was clear that he found the name unpleasant to pronounce.

"Are you Dr Waters?" Maurice asked; he had already resented the delay in the doctor's arrival sufficiently to pronounce his name with equal distaste.

"Yes, yes," said Dr Waters impatiently, "I'd better see this young woman as soon as possible."

"I'm her nephew," Maurice announced himself. "I think she's all right now."

"That's really for me to decide, old chap. It's far from what Miss Cherrill said. I suppose she's with the girl."

"No," Maurice said, "she's gone up to her room."

Dr Waters turned and grinned boyishly, "Well, I daresay we can get over that little loss," he said. "Lead the way, old chap, will you?"

Maurice indicated Sylvia's door. "If you don't mind I think I ought to look for my grandmother. I heard her voice outside."

"There's an old girl knocking daylight out of a taxi-driver," Dr Waters said, and he knocked on Sylvia's door. Maurice, wondering if the doctor were drunk, went out into the darkness.

There indeed was Mrs Liebig arguing with a taxi-driver. She had reacted to the emergency by putting on a pair of royal blue slacks, a short fur coat and a cyclamen silk scarf wound turbanwise around her head. It was the costume in which she had braved the air-raids, but as Maurice's memory did not go back to this time, he felt only acute embarrassment at her appearance.

When she saw her grandson, she called raucously, "Well, it's all right, my dear, he's going to wait." She came up the steps puffing and grumbling. "What do they think we are?" she asked. "Paupers? 'You'll get good money,' I told him. Ring for another taxi? What does he mean? I'll pay him to wait. I've got the money. 'Ring up and perhaps there aren't any more taxis,' I told him. 'I'm an old woman!' I told him. 'Do you think I want to wait about all night in a place like this?'."

Maurice said sharply, "Sylvia's been very ill. The doctor's with her now. She tried to kill herself but she only made herself sick."

"Well, there you are," Mrs Liebig said, "Victor should never have picked up with her."

"You've no need to worry about *him*," Maurice said bitterly. "He's left her for some other woman." And when he saw that his grandmother was about to defend her son, he interrupted violently, "He's lucky not to have a murder on his hands."

"Murder?" Mrs Liebig said. "Don't talk nonsense. You don't know what you are talking about. A boy of your age mixed up in all this. Where's her own people, anyway? What's her mother doing? My God, what a rotten world we live in."

At his grandmother's words, all Maurice's heroic mood shrivelled inside of him. He felt that he had simply muddled the whole affair; he had never inquired about Sylvia's parents. "She's very young," he said hesitatingly; he could think of nothing else to express what he felt for Sylvia.

"Young," Mrs Liebig echoed scornfully. "That's the trouble. A lot of children's nonsense, the lot of you. Well, where is the girl?" And when Maurice moved towards Sylvia's door, she pushed past him and brusquely forced her way in.

Sylvia was lying back on the pillows—a ghostlike little waif. To Maurice's eyes she seemed to have faded surprisingly far out of life in the short while he had been gone.

"Well," said Dr Waters, "she's going to be all right.

Aren't you, young woman? If she'd taken anything but aspirins she'd be dead. As it is I've given her an injection just to help nature along."

Maurice who was sceptical of the knowledge of general practitioners assumed the air of an educated mission schoolboy before the tribal witch doctor; but Mrs Liebig exclaimed knowingly, "Ah, there you are."

Dr Waters now assumed a stern look. "I need to know a bit more about all this, though. I'll have to examine the patient a bit further. I must ask you to wait outside," he announced.

"Yes, yes," Mrs Liebig cried, "you can't be here when doctor's examining her, Maurice. That wouldn't do at all." Maurice moved towards the door. "I'll call you when doctor's done," Mrs Liebig said.

Dr Waters swung on her angrily. "Will you kindly follow him. I want to talk to the young woman alone."

Mrs Liebig's face was crimson, "Don't you order me about," she cried, "I've no intention of leaving this girl in here with you."

It was Dr Water's turn to approach apoplexy. "I would remind you, Madame," he said, "that it may well be my duty to turn this matter over to the police, with unpleasant consequences for those responsible for this girl's welfare."

Mrs Liebig was too astonished to reply. Maurice looked for some contradiction of the doctor's innuendo from Sylvia, but she had only faded further away into the ghost world. "Now then," Dr Water's cried sharply. "Out with the lot of you."

In the passage Mrs Liebig gave it to Maurice good and

proper. "Can't you behave like a gentleman?" she
asked. "Good God! What would your father say? So
I've had to wait for my old age to watch my grandson
stand by and see me insulted. How do you know he's a
doctor?" she asked. "What's he doing in there with that
girl? They're pretty filthy, some of these doctors; I could
tell you stories. What does Victor think I am? To be at
the beck and call of every little tart he picks up off the
street—his own mother!" And so on.

Maurice said nothing; indeed he heard very little—his
thoughts were entirely upon Sylvia, a little puzzling at
her sudden languishing, but in the main just dwelling on
her.

It was over ten minutes before Dr Waters emerged
from the room. Mrs Liebig was already urging that they
should leave. "Let her stew in her own dirty juice," she
said. "She got what she was after with her tricks. Good
God! I should think Victor *has* left her, and if he never
takes up with her again, good riddance to bad rubbish."

Dr Waters cut into all this abruptly. "I think she'll be
all right now," he said, "I apologise if I seemed rude but
one must have a free hand in these affairs. I should like,"
he added, "someone to stay with her. She's still a little
hysterical, and I can't say that I'm surprised. Besides,
when that husband of hers comes back, heaven knows
what may happen. Can I rely on one of you to stop with
her?"

Mrs Liebig's expression was so unpromising that Dr
Waters seemed finally to decide on Maurice as his
assistant, despite his youth. He took him by the arm and
drew him aside, "If that brute comes back and pesters

her," he said, "you may tell him that I shall be over in the morning and that I shall have one or two very un-pleasant words to say to him. You can say," he chuckled sardonically, "that if he's so anxious for a thrashing he may well get it from an unexpected quarter. Filthy brute! Keep her quiet," he added. "Poor little creature!"

Before he left the house, he bowed to Mrs Liebig. "Good-night to you, Madam," he said. But she did not acknowledge his salute.

Back in the bedroom, Maurice had scarcely time to register the charm of Sylvia's wan smile, before the old crab-sidling woman came hobbling in. Like Dr Waters, she disregarded Mrs Liebig, so that Maurice began to wonder whether his grandmother's trousers, so unsuit-able to her age, had robbed her of all claim on public respect.

"Mr Morello wants to see you right away," the old woman mumbled to him.

"I shan't be a few minutes," he said to Mrs Liebig and, determined on his new authority, he was gone from the room before she could protest.

Mr Morello seemed also to accept Maurice's authority; indeed he appeared anxious to counter with a demon-stration of his own powers of command. He had changed his dressing-gown for a dark, rather too carefully 'city suit' and had seated himself at a large roll-topped desk which loomed incongruously in the obvious bed-sitting-room. His stature as landlord was asserted only in the neat divan bed and the unvarnished 'modernistic' wardrobe and chest-of-drawers—a setting two whole 'bed-sitter' social grades above the furnishings he provided for his tenants. Even to Maurice's eye Mr Morello seemed ill at ease in his authority. His plump young face was smooth with massage, the bluish stubble of his heavy jowl was carefully powdered; but on his neck was an angry boil and his fingers seemed unable to leave it alone.

"I'm afraid this can't go on, you know," he said. His voice was surprisingly light for so heavy a man; his accent was Birmingham.

Maurice looked round the room and sat down on the divan. "Of course, of course," Mr Morello said. He was clearly embarrassed at his failure as host. "You'll excuse this spot," he said, and when Maurice did not answer, he added in extenuation, "It's a boil, you know. There's nothing to do but wait for them to come to a head." Feeling that he had gone too far perhaps in excuses, he sat back in his swivel chair and folded his hands over his stomach. "I know things are difficult," he said with paternal pomposity. "It's a very bad time indeed for artists." He spoke with authority of a gamekeeper pronouncing on the partridge season. "We all get to the end of our tether at times. Some quite small trouble or other comes along and we break. I've felt like that with this boil." He laughed deprecatingly, but it was clear that he did not feel the irritation to be a small one. To Maurice he seemed so like a vulgar parody of his form master that he expected him to add, "But do *I* break down and try to commit suicide?"

Instead Mr Morello pushed out his thick underlip, looking like a sea elephant. "This house is a good part of my living," he announced, "and I can't have it getting a bad name. This sort of thing might easily lose me

tenants. Good tenants. Paying tenants," he added
ominously. "With all due allowance and having every
sympathy I hope, if it happens again they'll have to go.
Will you please tell Mrs Liebig that, when she's recovered
enough to face the facts of the situation." He paused and
then as though resolving the situation from superior
wisdom, he said, "It may well be a good thing to frighten
her a bit."

Maurice was annoyed at the man's patronising tone; he
felt dissatisfied too with his own lack of command over
the situation. He searched for some means of asserting
himself; then, "I think it was quite unnecessary of Miss
Cherrill to have shouted my aunt's private affairs about
the house."

Only his dislike of Mr Morello had made him speak
and he immediately expected a sharp rebuff, but the landlord only pouted like a fat, cross baby. "I don't want any
trouble with Miss Cherrill, please," he said pleadingly.
"She's a good, paying tenant. I'm sure I'm glad to have
made contact with one of Mrs Liebig's family," he
smiled. "It's a thousand pities she's had such bad luck.
There's money to be made in dancing to-day. Really
good dancing." He was clearly a man who prided himself
on knowing how things stood in the world of to-day.
"But there you are, accidents may happen to anyone."

Maurice could make nothing of this so he did not reply.

"Well," Mr. Morello cried cheerily, "she'll be all right
with you there, I can see." He got up and opened the
door for Maurice; he was clearly anxious to efface his
previous insufficient manners. "I feel a lot happier for
our little chat," he said. "You really must excuse me

receiving you in this state." Once more his fingers went
up to the boil on his neck. "If there's hot water or anything needed I'm sure Martha will be glad to oblige."

Mrs Liebig was standing in the hall when Maurice came
out. "Ah, good God, there you are," she cried, "do you
think I'm made of money? Keeping that taxi there all
night."

As though to underline her anxiety, the door-bell
buzzed loudly; and when Maurice opened it, there was
indeed the taxi-driver.

"All right, all right," Mrs Liebig cried, "I'm coming.
Do you think you're going to lose your money."

The little, greyfaced old taxi-driver seemed so cowed
by her that he only said, "Well, it's a long time, lady."

"A long time?" Mrs Liebig cried, "there's illness here;
of course it's a long time. Well, Maurice, are you ready?"

"I must stay here. The doctor asked me to." Maurice
tried to sound as casual as he could manage, but he felt,
though he could not explain why, that his whole future
happiness depended upon his getting his way about
this.

"Stay here? Good God! The girl's all right now.
Stay here? Of course you can't stay here with that girl
alone in her bedroom, a young man of your age. What
good would you be anyway, a boy like you?"

"The doctor . . ." Maurice began, but she broke in
furiously.

"What do we know about the doctor, anyway? You
and your doctors—you wait until you know a bit more
about life," she added darkly.

Maurice's thin face was tensed. "Either you or I must

stay," he said, "unless we're to risk a death on our hands." Perhaps it was the sibilance of his voice betraying to her his emotional state, or perhaps it was the fear that she might indeed have to stay; whatever the cause Mrs Liebig gave a hard little laugh. "All right," she cried, "I wash my hands. You and your morbid ideas. But *you* must explain to your mother. I hope you enjoy upsetting everybody like this, for that's what you're doing."

To Maurice's surprise she then went into Sylvia's room and, crossing to the bed, kissed the girl warmly on both cheeks. "Maurice is staying to see you're a good girl," she said. "Now, don't you worry. You're a good girl, even if you are a little fool. Victor'll find his luck again. You don't have to blame yourself. That Paula must give him a divorce. You'll see, it'll turn out all right. Oh, yes," she cried, turning to Maurice, "I know. Happy endings aren't good enough for your clever ways. It's all got to be deaths and suicides and wild ducks. But Sylvia isn't such a little fool as that. She'll be all right." She kissed the girl again.

Once more Maurice felt surprise, for Sylvia looked at Mrs Liebig with little girl's rounded eyes. "Thank you," she whispered gently, "you've been so very kind. You've helped me to believe again a little."

Mrs Liebig only said, "Now you sleep, my dear, and you let her sleep, Maurice."

Now that he was alone with Sylvia, Maurice was completely bewildered. He had asserted his right to remain on the stage, but of what the play was about he was entirely ignorant. For two years now, since his sixteenth birthday, he had been schooling himself to the sense of

authority, the power of command, the heroic role which
he and his friends in the Upper Sixth were determined to
assume. They had discussed it so often, schooled themselves for the task of leadership which would fall to their
generation—leadership out of the desert of the television
world, out of the even more degrading swamps of
espresso bar rebellion. They had fed themselves on high
purposes and self discipline, on gallantry and panache, on
Carlyle and Burke. Now for the first time he was called
upon to control a situation, however paltry the occasion,
and yet the situation seemed to drift by while he stood,
like a night stroller on the towing-path scarcely able to
distinguish water from land. He was emerging not as the
hero leader but as that feeble figure, the homme moyen
sensuel—the 'hero' type of all the literature that he and his
friends most despised. And he saw no way out of it.

Sylvia accepted his silence at first, lying back on her
pillows. With the eyes closed, her face seemed strangely
smooth and empty of life; she looked both older and lost.
Gradually her underlip protruded in a sulky pout and her
forehead wrinkled in a frown. To Maurice she now
appeared like a sullen, bored child; but as he could make
no sense of all that he had seen and heard of her, he tried
to ignore this new ugly impression that she made on him.
Suddenly the frown and the pout disappeared; opening
her eyes, she looked at him tragically. "Why do you
think God hates me so?" she asked.

A question based on so many doubtful premises
shocked Maurice deeply; such melodramatic speech from
such attractive lips disturbed him even more.

Sylvia sensed his disquiet, she let her hand fall on the

eiderdown in front of her in a gesture of hopelessness. "Oh God! always trying to find a way out, always trying to find someone else to put the blame on, even poor old God. Do you ever hate yourself like hell?" she asked.

This question was somewhat easier for Maurice to answer, although he found its formulation hardly more to his taste. "Quite often," he said. "I should think most people of any intelligence or feeling do at some time or other."

Sylvia seemed to ponder for a moment. "You understand things so well and yet you're so young," she said simply.

It was so exactly what Maurice had hoped to think of himself, and yet so exactly what he now doubted, that he looked at her covertly to see if she was speaking sarcastically; but her expression was one of childlike wonderment.

"How old are you?" she asked.

"Almost eighteen."

"Almost," she said, and she smiled. "That makes me terribly old. I'm twenty-three," she said.

"That's not old, really," Maurice tried not to sound a little disappointed.

"Almost eighteen and you know so much. I wish you could teach me some of it." Sylvia's wondering far-away voice would not have disgraced a performance of Marie Rose.

His age was not exactly what Maurice wished to harp upon, and her praise, though pleasing, was an indulgence high purpose did not allow him. "I'm afraid there isn't much point in our discussing these things unless you tell me why you wanted," he paused a moment and then, determinedly realistic, ended, "to kill yourself. Something Miss Cherrill said made me think . . ." he went on and then stopped again—to speak about pregnancy was embarrassing, but then Dr Waters' suggestion about Uncle Victor's depraved sexual tastes was an even less possible topic of conversation.

Sylvia's pupils contracted to two minute forget-me-nots. "What did Miss Cherrill say?" she asked, her husky voice now edgy.

"That you were going to have a baby . . ."

Maurice wished now that he had set about assuming control in a different way, but he was left little time to regret, for Sylvia burst out in fury, "That lying cow," she said. "Anyway, I've got a bloody sight better chance than her. No man would give her one. How dare she open her filthy mouth about my affairs? I'll have it out with her now." She began to lift herself with difficulty from the bed.

Maurice put his hand on her arm. "No," he said, "you must stay where you are. Perhaps I misunderstood her."

For whatever reason, Sylvia seemed willing to accept his restraint. "And if I *were* going to, as if I shouldn't know where to go to get rid of it. Better than that silly bitch would," she said and lay back on the pillows once more, smiling to herself.

Maurice's silence weighed down upon her satisfaction, however, and broke it. She turned to him angrily again, "You think I'm pretty sordid, don't you?" she asked.

"I wasn't making any judgment. I was just trying to understand, that's all," he replied. The words came out

K

automatically and he blushed not only for their priggish-ness but for their untruth—he *had* been thinking the whole episode sordid.

"Well, you *should* think it sordid—sordid and disgust-ing. For that's what it is. You've no idea of the foul things . . ."

"I think I have," Maurice said. "Dr Waters told me something."

Sylvia began to giggle. "What did *he* say?"

Maurice found this quite difficult; to begin with he wasn't quite sure if he had interpreted Dr Waters aright, and then he was also very uncertain if his interpretation might not be nonsense. He knew there were such sexual deviations, but applied to Sylvia and Victor it seemed absurd. He did not want to make a fool of himself.

"Come on," said Sylvia sharply. "What did he say?"

So urged, Maurice blurted it out crudely, "He said Victor made you beat him and that was why you'd . . ."

Sylvia, to his consternation, roared with laughter. "Dr Waters is a fool," she said. "Dr Waters made a pass, and that was naughty of Dr Waters, so Sylvia told him where he could put his pass."

It was, perhaps, the theatricality of her manner that suddenly decided Maurice. All his bewilderment suddenly vanished as a pattern formed before him. "That's not true. None of what you've been saying is true—to Dr Waters or to Morello or to Grandmother or to me. You just make up stories about yourself?"

Sylvia leaned quickly out of the bed and smacked his face. "You get out of here," she said, "go on, get out."

Maurice rose, there seemed nothing else to do but go.

He had not moved however, before she burst into tears.

"It's true," she cried. "Oh God! it's true. But what else is there to do when I'm so unhappy. That or get out of it, out of all this useless meaningless squalor. I'm so unhappy," she said again, "and so bored. What's the point of life? Oh, it's different for you . . ."

"No," said Maurice, "it isn't." And he told her of his own despair and boredom. She listened for a while like an attentive child, then she seemed to grow restless with her own silence. Once or twice she tried to break in but Maurice was intent on confiding his troubles. At last she cried, "Well then, if you feel like that, what's the hope for someone like me? You don't know what real dull respectability is like, or worse still this sort of sordid disreputable life."

Then in her turn she told her story—a more vivid recitation than Maurice's. The large family, the dead drudgery of the Luton newspaper shop her parents owned, running away to London, film extra work, Woolworth's soap counter, hostess at a little club, Victor.

It was at once a story so familiar to Maurice from what he had read in the newspapers, and so personal from her vivid narration, that he was spellbound. He only interrupted her once, "And prison?" he asked.

"Oh! the whole thing's a prison," she cried.

"Is all this true that you're telling me?" he demanded.

"No, I shouldn't have said that. Only it's all so difficult."

"Oh, yes, you should," she replied. "How can you believe me when I've told you so many lies. But it *is* true. Not what I've said before. That about prison was just to make myself interesting. It wasn't even true about Victor. He hasn't been unfaithful. He just didn't come back to-night because it's all so hopeless. He feels he can't help me and he's right, nobody can. I'm no use."

It was now Maurice knew that he ought to convince her of what life could be, *was* going to be when his generation got their chance, but he found himself taking advantage of a quite different chance. He got up and kissed her. When he found that she lay so passive in his embrace, his shyness left him and he kissed her excitedly if a little clumsily on mouth and cheeks, ears and neck. She lay purring like a white cat that has found warmth.

"It's nice," she said in her husky voice, "we're both young and that's right, isn't it?"

He had hardly started to stroke her arms again a little clumsily before she seemed to become drowsy. Then she pushed him away—but gently.

"No," she said, "it's no good. Victor and I belong to each other. It may be hell but that's the way it is." Maurice noticed for the first time that her voice had assumed a faint American note. "Victor and I are down-hillers," she said. "You're not. Look," she went on, "I like you. You understand so much and you've helped. I need a friend who I can talk to. Will you be my friend?"

Maurice could not remember feeling so depressed, but he summoned all his courage to assent.

"I want to sleep now," she said. "And you must go, because if Victor comes back he'll be worried if you're here and I'm too tired to face any more trouble."

"The doctor said . . ." Maurice began.

"Please, don't make it worse."

"All right," Maurice said, "but you won't be silly again."

"Cross my heart," she said. "Come and see me again. I like to hear you talk."

Maurice moved to the door. "Of course, I shall come to-morrow to see how you are."

Sylvia seemed to hesitate, then she smiled lazily, "Okay," she said, "but don't come before five. I'm going to have a lovely long sleep," and she curled down among the grubby sheets and blankets.

Maurice could find no taxi until he reached Marble Arch and by that time he was so absorbed in trying to sort out his emotions that he preferred to walk home.

He too slept long and heavily. Mrs Liebig was already lunching when he woke. She seemed anxious at first that he should have been involved in last night's trouble. "I don't know what to say to Norman," she said. "He ought to be pleased that you did so much for his brother's girl. But heaven knows what your mother may say. I can't tell their ideas. Better say nothing. Yes, that's it," she cried, "tell them nothing. Do you hear, you're to tell them nothing. All the same you behaved well, Maurice."

When she found that he ate a good lunch, she seemed less worried. "Victor's got in a fine mess," she said. "All the same it's his life. That Paula must give him a divorce. I shall tell her. She's got a good job; what's she want to hang on to him for?" But when Maurice asked her if she had arranged to see Aunt Paula, she answered vaguely. "Time enough," she said. "Besides it's all nonsense. You're not to think anymore of it, do you hear? At your age. There's quite enough with your wild ducks. All that

Sylvia and Victor. It's a lot of nonsense. It's just the way they live." And with that she dismissed the subject. She was more intent that he should meet her on time for *The Pajama Game*.

Maurice found himself near Westbourne Grove long before five o'clock, but he passed the time impatiently in a tea room. When at last five o'clock sounded from a near-by church, he ran all the way to Sylvia's house for fear that she might be annoyed at his lack of punctuality. When Sylvia opened the door, his fears seemed to be realised, for she scowled at him. Her appearance in day-light surprised him; she was shorter than he had expected, and as a result her plumpness seemed a little gross. Her breasts reared at him aggressively through her tight white sweater and her hips seemed almost tyre-like beneath her tighter black skirt. Heavy, bright lipstick made her cheeks seem waxen. Her fair hair fell loosely across her forehead. All in all, however, she sharpened his desire.

"Oh! hullo," she said a little crossly. "I'm nearly ready. You'd better come in while I finish my face. Victor's expecting us at the club."

In the bedroom she put on an Elvis Presley record on the gramophone and sat before the mirror doing her eye-brows. Maurice tried to make conversation but her in-attention and the deafening volume of 'Blue Suede Shoes' made it impossible. He sat on the bed and stared dis-consolately into the distance. When at last she had finished, he met her turning glance with a smile. She smiled in return and stopped the record, "Elvis the pelvis," she said, but there seemed to be no possible reply.

"It's only a little drinking club," she announced, "but we always go there." Before they left the house, she added, "It was sweet of you to come round."

The club was up three flights of bare wooden stairs and very dark when you entered. The radiogram here was playing Dickie Valentine. There were only three people sitting at the bar and none of them was Victor.

"Hullo, Sylvia," the barman said, and a thin dark girl cried, "Sylvia, darling!"

"Hullo," said Sylvia, "I expected Victor."

"He's gone to the little boy's room," said the girl. "He'll be back in a jiffy."

"This is Maurice," Sylvia said. "Maurice, meet Joy and Davy. King of his own frontier," she added and laughed depressedly.

"What's it to be?" Davy asked.

"Gin," said Sylvia. "Gin and what, Maurice?"

But Maurice was seized with panic. He must be gone before Victor returned. "I really think I'll have to go," he said, "I've got to be at the theatre."

"Oh God!" cried Sylvia, "do you really go to the theatre? It's ghastly."

"I haven't been to the theatre for years," Joy announced. "We always go to the pictures."

"I'm afraid I must go, though," Maurice said.

"Well, yours was a quick one all right," Davy said.

Just as Maurice was stumbling out on to the top step in the darkness, he found Sylvia beside him. "I'm being bloody, I know," she said, "but that's how it has to be." Once more her accent was American. "I do need your friendship though. More than you know. I can't go on with it all much longer, even for Vic's sake. Can I call on you to help if things get too bad?"

Maurice was afraid of falling down the stairs, so it was with difficulty that he said, "Yes, of course."

"It may be sooner than you think. It may be to-night," Sylvia answered and kissed him on the mouth. Then she went back into the club room. Maurice stumbled down the stairs.

All the way back in the taxi from *The Pajama Game* Mrs Liebig hummed 'Fernandos Hideaway'. "That was a good show," she said. "Something to take away with you." She was tired, however, and had her nightcap in bed. Maurice sat up and read Burke's Chivalrous challenge to arms in defence of the fair, unhappy Queen of France. He found it difficult, however, to feel sufficiently for Marie Antoinette's wrongs and once or twice he half rose from his chair, thinking that he had heard the ring of the telephone.

Higher Standards

"COME along then, both," said Mrs Corfe. It had been the form of her call to tea at half-past six every evening for more than fifteen years. Perhaps it had lost some of its accuracy since Mr Corfe's stroke some four years before, but home would not have been the same without it; and, if Mrs Corfe's conception of 'home' was a trifle ill-defined, her determination that it should never be other than 'the same' was the central thread of all her actions and words.

There was nothing to upset her mother's love of sameness in her daughter's slow response to her call. It merely meant that Elsie had come home in one of her moods. There was a time, of course, before the war when Elsie had not had 'moods'. Indeed, there was a sort of tacit agreement between mother and daughter that the blackness of these moods should be indicated by the length of time that Elsie remained in her bedroom after the summons to meals. If, as on that evening, Mrs Corfe had time to hoist her husband from his chair and support him doll-like on his dangling legs to the loaded table, before her daughter appeared at the foot of the stairs peering myopically with refined distaste at the jelly and the jam puffs, then it was clearly one of Elsie's bad evenings. Not that this particularly distressed Mrs Corfe, for it allowed her to say brightly, "Waiting for late folk never made an egg fresher or the tea hotter."

Elsie's rejoinder to the implied moral rebuke was æsthetic. She carefully removed one by one from the overcrowded table the many half empty pots of jam and bottles of sauce without which her mother felt the evening meal to be incomplete. Then, going to the mirror, she set the little lemon *crêpe de Chine* scarf she wore in the evenings into pretty artistic folds; she further asserted her more refined canons of taste by loosening the beech leaves in the vase on the mantelpiece. Such autumn decoration was the sole incursion on the more traditional furnishing of the parlour that her rebellion had ever achieved. Her mother's revenge came each morning when she crammed the branches back into the vase.

Boiled eggs in egg-cups shaped like kittens and roosters were followed by a 'grunter', a traditional local dish to which, under the stress of rationing, Mrs Corfe had become increasingly attached. Originally designed as a baked suet roll to contain strips of pork or bacon, it had become a convenient receptable for all unattractive scraps. Mrs Corfe, however, retained the humour of the tradition by inserting two burnt currants for the pig's eyes and a sprig of parsley for its tail.

Elsie, like her mother in so many things, shared her love of quaint local customs; but the 'grunter' was a whimsy against which her stomach had long revolted at the end of a tiring day's teaching. She selected three brussel-sprouts and, cutting them very exactly into four parts each, chewed them very carefully with her front teeth. Mrs Corfe ate heartily, continually spearing fresh pieces of the 'grunter' with her knife. The noise of her mother's feeding brought to Elsie's pale features a fixed expression of attention to higher things.

Neither her daughter's aura of self-pity nor her own preoccupation with feeding in any way inhibited Mrs Corfe's continous flow of talk. After a day of housework and sick nursing, she looked forward to her daughter's return with a greed that was almost physical. To scatter the weariness and frustration of life's daily round in an evening's censorious gossip, to indulge herself in little disapproving jokes about less thrifty, less respectable neighbours seemed the least that so many years of godly living and duty and deadening physical labour might be expected to give to a tired old woman. It was perhaps her only real grudge against Elsie that the girl refused to apply to her jaded nerves the sharp restorative of a little vinegary talk about her neighbours. How soon these black moods would pass from her daughter, she reflected, if only she would allow herself the soothing easement of village scandal or discharge the heavy burdened soul in a righteous jibe or two.

"Carters have refused to serve 'The Laurels' again," she said. "The woman's half distracted. It's nice enough to have grand folk from London coming for the week-end; it's another thing to feed them from an empty larder. Oh!" she drew in her breath with disapproving relish. "The woman's been on the telephone all day to the other shops. She'll make use of *that* at any rate until it's cut off. But for any effect it's had, she might have saved her breath. On *one* tradesman's black books, on *all*. There might be a pint of milk and a plate of porridge for the city folks *if* they're lucky," she paused for a second and then added, "And there might not. But still she's got her fur coat to keep her warm outside, if there's no soup to cheer the inner man."

Elsie tried hard not to envy Mrs Hardy her musquash. She pictured as vividly as she could the vulgarity, the terrible, clashing bright colours of the drawing-room at 'The Laurels' when she attended the Red Cross committee meetings there. But it was no good, she wanted the fur coat.

Mrs Corfe tried another tack. If the punishment of the godless brought no comfort, then the distresses of the back-sliding would surely answer.

"It's been a day of wonders at the Fitchett's," she announced with mock solemnity. "At eight o'clock our Bess had won ten thousand on the Pools. It was *pounds* then, but when the morning post brought nothing, it was down to shillings. All the same the old man quite bit Miss Rennett's head off when she mentioned principles. Nothing against Pools in The Book, it seems. But when the afternoon post went by, there was quite a change around. Nasty, ungodly things the Pools. Mrs Fitchett's given our Bess a talking to, so we'll have *her* yellow bonnet back in Chapel next Sunday. Ah! well, it takes more than the Fitchetts and such turnabouts to change the ways of old Nick."

Elsie remembered the lecture she had given to Standard Four only that morning against gambling. Television and Pools and Space Robots, that was all the children of to-day thought about. But somewhere at the back of her vision a tall, dark stranger leaned over to loosen her sable wrap for her as she settled herself in the gondola.

"How heavenly St Mark's looks to-night," she said with exquisite taste, and, "*Our* St Mark's," he replied.

Of course, the Pools were a terrible drain on the nation's decency, but . . .

Mrs Corfe was playing her last card now in the macabre vein. She had almost finished the jelly, and soon it would be time to put Father to bed, so there was not a moment to lose if the evening was to bring any cosy exchange.

"They doubt," she said, "if old Mary will last the night. The poor old soul's been wandering terribly, and bringing up every scrap she's taken. . . ."

But Elsie had endured enough of the sordid aspects of life. She leaned across the table, speaking very distinctly:

"And what did *you* do to-day, Father?" she asked.

A twitch of anger shot through Mrs Corfe's wrinkled cheek. Now that *was* selfish of Elsie, selfish and thoughtless. Her father who had been such a fine man, so hardworking and thrifty, and such a splendid lay preacher, too, for all that he'd had no education. What had he *done* to-day, indeed? What *could* he do since this wicked thing had struck him? And what indeed could *she* do but keep him neat and clean before their neighbours as he would have wished.

"Well, gel," Mr Corfe replied, "I sat up at back window and watched the fowls. It's a wonder the way that crookity-backed one gets the scraps. Why should *she* have had the crooked back, I asked myself. Oh, the ways of Providence are strange: all they fowls and only one crookity backed, and yet she gets her share. There's a thing to think upon, and to talk upon . . ."

"Yes, yes, indeed," said Mrs Corfe, "but not now." It shamed her that her husband who had always been so clear in his thoughts, so upstanding, should at last wander so unsuitably in his words. Elsie, too, felt the need to protect her father from what his failing body had made him; and so, when her mother began to question her on the events at school that day, she forced herself to answer.

"It's been a Standard IV day for you I know, my girl, by your tired looks," said Mrs Corfe. And when Elsie began to recount the exploits of that famous undisciplined class, her mother listened avidly. Such sad happenings, such examples of human frailty in the nearby town, were second only to village misdemeanours in her catalogue of pleasures.

"Ah! the Mardykes, I thought they'd be somewhere in it. There's a couple of old Nick's own that'll come to sorry ends," she said with fervour, when Elsie mentioned the notorious bad boys of the form. "And the woman had sent them out with nothing but a rumble in their stomachs for breakfast, I'll be bound." It was the fecklessness of city workers that so fascinated Mrs Corfe. And then, as though her bitterness had sated itself, she added, "You must take them some apples to-morrow, Elsie. They're a couple of comics if ever there were any."

"Miss Teasdale's away with the flu," said Elsie, "so I've got *her* handful to deal with, too."

"And why can't they get a Supply in?" asked her mother impatiently.

"Supply teachers need notification. Why do you use words you don't understand?" Elsie asked angrily.

It was lucky that noises in the village street came so suddenly to prevent a family quarrel. Shrill whistles could be heard, loud shouting, the sharp swerve of bicycle wheels followed by guffaws of coarse laughter.

"H'm," said Mrs Corfe. "Well, there's *our* Standard IV anyway." It was their favourite name for the youths who nightly rode the length of the village street to call after girls.

Half an hour later when Elsie went to the pillar-box with a letter to an old friend of her Teacher's Training College days, a group of these young men were leaning on the nearby fence. Well! she thought, Bill Daly and Jim Soker among them, they ought to be ashamed wasting their time like that. At their age, too. Why, Jim was a year older than herself, quite twenty-six. She was about to pass by with her usual self-conscious, majestic disregard, when her loneliness was shot through with an aching for those childhood days before awakening prudery and her scholarship to the 'County' had cut her off from the village Standard IV. She paused for a moment at the pillar-box and looked back at them. One of the younger boys let out a wolf whistle, but Bill Daly stopped him short.

"Hallo, Elsie," he said in the usual imitation American, "how about a little walk?"

The retort came easily to Elsie's lips, "Does teacher know you're out of school, Bill Daly?" she said; but the words came strangely—not in her customary school-marm tone, but with a long-buried, common, cheeky giggle. She even smiled and waved, and her walk as she left them was almost tarty in its jauntiness. She was tempted to look back, but another wolf whistle recalled her to her superior taste, her isolated social position in the village.

Mrs Corfe had her old black outdoor coat on, when Elsie returned.

"Who was that you were talking to?" she asked.

"Oh! Standard IV," Elsie answered, "Bill Daly was there. He ought to be ashamed fooling about like that at his age."

"Well, it's lucky there are folks with *higher* standards," said her mother. "Father's not too good," she added, "the 'grunter's' turned on him. I'm just off down to old Mary's. I've promised to sit with the poor creature. It may help to keep the bogies away."

Elsie's outing seemed to have softened her mood. She touched her mother's arm. "You do too much for them all," she said.

"Oh! well," Mrs Corfe replied gruffly, "if the poor won't help the poor, I'd like to know who will. I don't like leaving your father though. . . ."

Through the flat acceptance of their life implied in her mother's tone came once more the wolf whistles and guffaws, and mingled with them now the high giggle of the village girls. Elsie's laugh was hard and hysterical. "Oh! don't fuss, so, mother," she cried, "I'll sit up with father. You haven't got a monopoly of higher standards, you know."

A Sad Fall

MRS TANNER stood in the porch watching the hired car disappear down the drive taking her son to the London train—first short lap of his long journey overseas. She waved once or twice; but it was not Jeremy's face that turned to smile at her, only Naomi's, so she bent her heavy body ostentatiously to examine the loose paving in the front steps. Her sudden attention to the cracked paving would make clear her deliberate rejection of the smile, for her daughter-in-law knew well enough that the dilapidation of the house was one of the things that least concerned her. It was surely enough that she shared this war-time rural isolation with Naomi, had allowed her to go alone with Jeremy for his embarkation; she had earned a right to a single act of rudeness to this stranger brought in by marriage. In any case Naomi was well aware of the mutual indifference upon which their friendly relationship rested.

From the drawing room came the sound of a piano duet. Mozart or Beethoven—Mrs Tanner made no attempt to guess. Music was not one of the cultural horizons which her isolation and ill health had extended. Even her uninclined ear, however, noted Roger's stumbling treble in contrast to John Appleby's practised bass.

She felt a now rare sense of pleasure in anticipating John's continued stay in her house. The weakening of once agonising maternal love was not all that old age brought in compensation for its other more depressing physical weaknesses; for the first time for many years she had found real delight in the company of a stranger. He had become one of those few whom she could put trust in if she had a sudden seizure; in her new diabetic scheme of life such people were the elect. Of course, an attentive audience of any sort was relief to the imprisonment of solitude. Then too John Appleby was not truly a stranger, but a wanderer returned from the happy lost days of Jeremy's youth. Nevertheless she knew that it was not just 'company' nor the past that had attracted her to the young man during his week's visit. Going into the hall lobby to leave the light tweed overcoat which the cold September afternoon had demanded, Mrs Tanner gave an unwonted glance to the dusty mirror and patted her white shingled hair into place on each side of her plump wrinkled cheeks. A look of almost coy merriment tempered the usual self-mourning gaze of her spaniel brown eyes as she went upstairs to take her insulin dose before joining the others in the drawing-room.

In that room Roger crashed his square topped fingers down on to the keys. "It's no good" he cried, I can't keep it up. You see I haven't kept my practising going this holiday," and he broke into a long giggling laugh that seemed oddly hysterically edged in so stolid and square framed a boy.

"Yes," said John Appleby, "I do see." His smile took from his deliberate tones their touch of rebuke. He got up from the piano stool and, crumbling his long thin body into an armchair, he began to fill his pipe.

The boy swung round on the other stool—a revolving one which he had brought to the piano from the desk in the dining-room. Legs apart, he drummed with his fingers on the stool's edge. He looked towards John, his lower lip pouting a little as though he feared his refusal to continue the duet had brought the conversation to an end. But John, as he sucked at his pipe, looked up at him over the bowl and between his suckings asked: "Do you give up with most of your prep like that?"

His note was schoolmasterly, but this must have been long accepted between them, for Roger said, "Yes, Professor," and laughed. "I get bored when things are difficult," he added.

"Or you think you do," John observed.

"I do," Roger repeated, the touch of petulance under-lined the cockney strain in his speech.

"So Tompkins is top of the form and not you. But you manage to get moved up each term, so why worry?" John's smile was quizzical. Roger's cheeks flushed, their high colour spreading up to the edge of his smoothly brilliantined fair hair. John's quizzical smile spread across his thin, monkey like face. He shook his head, "No, no, I mean it," he said, "it's the perfect recipe for sensible moderate success."

If there was an undertone to the gay, friendly note of his voice, it was beyond the range of the boy's thirteen years. He swung round again on the stool, his plump bare knees catching the light as he moved. He began to play 'Chopsticks' then changed to 'The March of the Tin

Soldiers'. "I had a hen and she laid such eggs that I gave her trousers for her legs," he sang. He bawled the words at the top of his voice.

Mrs Tanner, coming into the room, took in the boy's high spirits and smiled across at John. "Heavens what a noise!" she cried. The boy stopped singing, but continued to play the tune. "He's been lecturing me," he called over his shoulder.

"I made an observation," John said, "Roger took it as a rebuke."

"It wasn't an observationem," the boy threw back, "it was a jawing."

"No doubt deserved," Mrs Tanner concluded, "however little you liked it."

Roger refused the conclusion; "Oh, but I did like it," he said and swung round again, facing them rather primly, "I don't mind a bit with him."

"And I thought you were busy with your Mozart," Mrs Tanner said.

"Beethoven," John pretended to mutter, but cast a teasing look at her.

"Don't you make any of your observations to me, Mr Appleby," she cried. Then, deflecting the conversation from herself, "You mustn't take up all Mr Applebys time, Roger, he's got his paper to write."

"Oh my poor paper," John said, "you bring it in like a penance, Mrs Tanner. A hundred Hail Marys."

"Well I don't like the idea of an old woman and a schoolboy coming between you and a certain vague number." She brought out the technical phrase with a certain coquetry.

"Good Heavens. You've remembered it. I beg you not to clutter your head with such awful stuff."

"It might displace some of the useless lumber," Mrs Tanner said, "there's precious little else there."

"Oh, no, just the whole of Gibbon and *The Ring and the Book* and *Clarisa*."

"I wish I'd never told you about my war-time reading," Mrs Tanner replied, "it was simply a solitary old woman's chance of repairing a bit of her abysmal ignorance. In any case," she went on, "I thought scientists and mathematicians weren't interested in human beings of any sort let alone old women and schoolboys."

"We live among them," John smiled, "we must learn to deal with them. Otherwise we should leave it all to humanists like Hitler."

"Hitler was vilely inhuman."

"It's the same thing upside down. Too much attachment."

Mrs Tanner could not make nothing of it, but if she intended to voice her perplexity she was prevented by Roger. "I bet Hitler isn't dead really," he cried, "Is he? You know about it, don't you, Mr Appleby, that's your job spying."

"Now, Roger, I've told you you're not to question Mr Appleby about his job."

"But I'm not questioning him, Mrs Tanner. I'm just telling him he's a spy. Anyway what's clever about spying? I'll spy on you to-day, Mr Appleby, and you won't know I'm doing it."

John spoke in a heavy German accent, "Good morning, General Hannay," he said, "I did not recognise you at first in those grey flannel knickers." Roger gave way once more to his giggling laughter.

"General Hannay," Mrs Tanner said firmly, "must set the table for luncheon. You and I will have to share the chores, Roger, while Mrs Jeremy's in London. We usually have a roster of three," she explained to John.

"Oh, there's plenty of time," Roger said.

"No there is not. I've taken my insulin. I shall want my food sharp at one."

The boy's face assumed a look of reverence. Mrs Tanner's diabetes involved holy rituals. "I'll go straight away," he said, "is it fish?"

"Yes," Mrs Tanner laughed, I'm afraid it *is* fish, Roger."

As the boy opened the door to leave, he turned to John. If he seemed for a moment coy it was no more than the coquetry their visitor inspired in Mrs Tanner. "If I promise to practise will you take me to the cinema to-morrow, Mr Appleby?" he asked.

"I'll take you to the cinema, but without any promises. We don't appease any more, you know, in our brave new world," John said, and then, as though in fear that his moralising had offended the boy, he added, "Who knows we might see a Gumbleduck."

Whatever the intimacy offered, Roger did not receive it well. "How could we?" he asked, and went out of the room.

Mrs Tanner let herself down into a deep armchair, slowly filling its every crevice with her bulging flesh. She took up some sewing from the side table. "I hope you realise what you're letting yourself in for," she said.

"There'll be only Roger and me to talk to in the whole place." She waved her hand, incongruously small for her fat body, around the sitting room to indicate the vast spaces in which he was to be bored.

It was in fact, John Appleby reflected, only a moderate sized room in a smallish house with a smallish garden, less than half the size of the house the Tanners had occupied when he had visited them in his adolescence, yet she habitually spoke as though she was the unwilling mistress of a large estate. With his usual methodical approach to human behaviour, he sought an answer to the paradox and guessed that a house without servants seemed vast to her in the work it imposed.

He smiled with the teasing gallantry he had come to use with her. "I like talking to *Roger* very much," he said, "He's both sensible and ordinary. An extremely pleasant combination in a small boy."

Mrs Tanner, playing her part, pretended not to notice the teasing omission. "I'm so glad you like him," she said, "you're certainly very good with him. Not that he's at all difficult. I can't tell you how pleased Naomi and I were that out of all the evacuees he should be the only one who hasn't drifted back to London. I oughtn't to say it, of course, because, poor child! its dreadful that his Mother shouldn't want him. But from the very start he gave me no trouble. I suppose, as you say, he is a very ordinary boy. He'll never set the world on fire, but then the others only set the *house* on fire or lied or wetted their beds. Not a very pleasing sort of extraordinariness and certainly not the sort that an old woman of seventy wants to cope with. All the same, Roger or no Roger, I warn you that the house will be no place for an intelligent man to spend his leave in, you've only seen it when Jeremy and Naomi were here you don't know how dead it can be."

"I can't remember," he answered, "that Jeremy showed any sign this week of wanting to talk to anyone but Naomi, or Naomi for that matter of noticing anyone but him. She put up the better show of pretending, of course, but then I'm not *her* old school-friend. But they were neither of them aching to be sociable. All the same as far as I remember I've had a great deal of very pleasant conversation and it hasn't all been with Roger."

Mrs Tanner laughed but once again she disregarded the compliment, "They're terribly in love," she cried, "you must forgive them, *I* try to even though he is my son. As a matter of fact," she said, "old age and infirmity free one from a lot of encumbrances and one of them is an excessive mother love." She had bent over her sewing so that John speculated whether she was hiding a face that could belie her assured tone. "I can honestly say that I was glad to let Naomi go alone to see him off in London," she said emphatically, "I've ached for him at times during these war years, of course; after all he is my only one and I worry too when he's been in London during air raids. But I live much more with a past Jeremy now than with the real one. That's one of the reasons I've been so pleased to get to know you. You're a link with his past. Of course, its only *one* of the reasons," she added with a smile.

It was John's turn gracefully to ignore the compliment, "I hope you're not worried about his going to Calcutta,"

he said, "he'll be in less danger there, you know, than
he was in London."

"Oh heavens," she cried, "I'm not so blindly selfish
that I'm unaware of the enormous luck we have had that
he should be doing this intelligence work, whatever it is."
She threw him an amused glance; it was one of the
customary jokes of their friendship that she should be a
little arch about the secret work that he and Jeremy were
engaged in. "Oh no, he's safe enough. I feel quite guilty
about it at times. One of the few compensations of my
isolation down here is not having to face the other poor
women whose wretched men are *not* safely in Intelligence.
Naomi feels it at the hospital. So many of the nurses are
married or engaged to pilots. Perhaps Jeremy's going to
Calcutta will at least give her the peace of conformity
with the others."

John raised his eyebrows slightly, Mrs Tanner put
down her sewing and, removing her amber rimmed
spectacles, she turned her large, anxious yellow flecked
brown eyes upon him. "No, I don't mean it like that.
Not even unconsciously, I'm sure of it. I really *don't*
grudge her Jeremy's love." She stroked the pale lemon
silk of the cushion cover she was sewing as for a moment
she pondered. "Of course, I can't help remembering that
she will have Jeremy again in a world of peace and decency.
While as for me, a fat diabetic old woman—who can say
how long this awful Japanese war will last? But it's not
really him I'm thinking of. I've honestly and truly let
him go. No it's of myself. Oh, I know it's only a vege-
table life I live down here and it'll never be much more.
But to have got through this awful time, to have seen the

horror fade away in Europe. For I'm sure it will. And
then to face years more of it. I'm sorry I can't believe in
this far Eastern war or the necessity for it. I want so much
to see a world of gentleness again. That's why," she
smiled, "I've loved your courtesy in bothering with me
and Roger. You're so gentle in a violent, hurrying world."

"Oh," John exclaimed, "I'm civil enough, I suppose."
He ran his hand through his long black hair, pulling his
head down to the chairback so that his high cheek-boned
white face stared out at her against the dark red fabric.
"I shouldn't," he added, "put much trust in a world of
gentleness again though. It'll take an age to teach
manners again—if they *ever* come back."

This time Mrs Tanner's brown eyes showed no gleam,
they were all hurt spaniel, Charles I, reproach.

"Oh, it's more than manners that we need. It's love."

John, pipe between his teeth, ventured no more than,
"Ah?"

"Oh, yes," Mrs Tanner appealed, "surely. I know
something about it. You see," now her eyes seemed old
pools of wisdom, "I used to love possessively, holding
tight—husband, son, a London house I was proud of.
Well, I lost them all. Or at least I lost Oliver, and then
my health went, and the meaning of my life in London
went from me. I think I learnt then that holding tight
could only hurt me and others. That was why I was able
to let Jeremy go. And as to personal possessions—well,
you see the state of this house and the garden! I allow
them to be no more than somewhere I live in, some place
where I can take the air. Of course," she laughed, "I
can't do much else anyway with only a charwoman and

no gardener. But all the same," she changed to the serious with a degree of ostentation, "I have learned a little at last of how to love, I think, to love without holding."

Again John gave only the slightest interrogative, "Ah?"

"It's allowed me, for example, to be good friends with Naomi, simply because she's the woman my son loves." Provided with no comment, Mrs Tanner drew to her conclusion quickly. "Well, anyway that's the way the world has got to learn to love if we're ever to be done with all these horrors. And I think it will."

The fitful, yet strong September sunshine had lit upon John's chalkwhite furrowed forehead. Mrs Tanner took it as a way out of her one sided conversation. "Shall we seize the sunshine while it lasts?" she asked, "If, that is, you don't mind walking at a fat old woman's slow pace."

"We've talked so much about me and so little about you," Mrs Tanner remarked, as they walked at indeed a very slow pace across the ill-kept lawn, "women and especially old inquisitive women can be such a nuisance that I have purposely not asked questions. But that doesn't mean I'm not curious, of course I am."

"A lecturer in Mathematics at Oxford," John replied, "Educated at Shrewsbury with Jeremy Tanner. The best of educations surely?"

"Oh, indeed," Mrs Tanner laughed, "my father was headmaster of the school, you know. I always felt it had gone down by the time Jeremy went there. But then I was bound to."

"Well," he went on, "what else is there? Born in Brighton thirty-two years ago, father a stock-broker.

Oh, and, of course, engaged twice but never married."

If he supposed that the romantic note was what Mrs Tanner was waiting for, he seemed to be wrong, for she exclaimed impatiently, "Oh, I know all that. But were you happy as a child? I'm sure you must have been, and yet no woman can quite believe it about other people's children. And sometimes you seem so silent."

"I'm sorry," John laughed, I'm usually listening."

"Oh, you're a wonderful listener, who else would have allowed me to go on about my wretched diabetes as you have? Oh it's absurd of me, of course; you're bound to be abstracted with your brain, but you're so kind and put up such a show of interest that when for a moment you're not absolutely with one it seems strange."

John reached over and began to free a tall head of Michaelmas daisy from the bindweed that entangled it.

"Oh, if you once begin," Mrs Tanner said, "there'll be no end to it. Look at it, what a wilderness." And indeed the herbaceous border seemed a mass of weed—docks, polygonum, thistles and, over all, bindweed—only the Michaelmas daisies still fought a losing battle. "I warned you," she cried, "I've just let it all go. I can manage a few roses but for the rest I've let it go— and it's released me. Old age must beware of property." John too released the daisy and it swayed back to its weedy height.

"And they loved you, your parents?" Mrs Tanner asked.

"They were ideal," John replied, "We respected each other. They helped me to grow up and then, just when I had, they died."

For a moment Mrs Tanner could make nothing of it,

then she cried, "There! I knew it. I'm never wrong.
You *were* loved. Good, gentle, friendly people always
have been. It's the one thing I'm proud to have given
Jeremy—a loved childhood and . . ." But once again
her thoughts led on to silence. Then as the grass path
passed between the rhododendrons of the shrubbery out
on to a meadow, she said, "Well, there it is. Our famous
view. You said you liked it yesterday when it was
clouded in mist, but now you can see what the mist hid.
The vague red and grey to the left is Ludlow. And there
you have Wenlock Edge. And beyond you're supposed
to see The Long Mynd and on to the Welsh hills. And
so you could I suppose if Wenlock Edge was not so high."
She had a number of such little jokes to express her love-
hatred of her home of exile.

"As a matter of fact, I think I can," John said.

"Oh, I don't believe it. And if you can, what do you
see but a faint dark shape. And they call that *seeing* the
Welsh hills." Nevertheless she was pleased. She turned
back to the shrubbery, striking at the struggling arms of
rhododendrons with her ashplant. "Is this seat too wet?"
she asked, but before he could answer, she had sat down.
"Don't ever get fat." she said, "or rather don't get too
fat, for you could do with some extra weight."

Before John sat down next to her, he carefully folded
the mackintosh he was carrying and made a cushion for
himself. "I was really interested about the diabetes, you
know," he said.

"Oh, my dear boy!" Mrs Tanner exclaimed, "all the
same I'm sure you're right, it began with the shock of
Oliver's death."

"Its only a hypothesis."

Mrs Tanner, however, would have no modifications. "And none of those wretched doctors have seen it."

"It wouldn't have helped really, if they had, would it? It couldn't have brought your husband back."

"It always helps to know that our wretched bodies are under the control of our minds," Mrs Tanner declared, "it's a great comfort."

John smiled, "The modern world should hold great comfort for you then" he said.

"No," she went on, "your understanding of that has given me even more confidence in you. You see, every illness brings its fears and, although, of course, it's quite irrational, the only thing I fear is having one of those dreadful seizures when people are around whom I don't trust. It's quite absurd as I say, because it's only a question of regular meals, and if I go out I carry some sugar with me just in case. All the same there's some people I have confidence in. Roger, for instance, although he's only a small boy and now you, but not, I'm afraid, Naomi."

John took out his pipe and knocked it on the wooden bench. "You say these things about Naomi, and yet what I so admire is your friendly relationship with her. It can't be easy for two women together for all these years—and anxious years."

"Oh, it's not so bad. Of course she's difficult at times, but then so am I. She comes back from the hospital tired and then she tells me everything she's going to do. 'I'm just going to put on a kettle for the hot water bottles, Mother', or 'I'm only going upstairs for some wool,

Mother'. As if I wanted to know. But there, as you say, two women living together."

"That's interesting," John observed, then he said by way of solution, "she probably needs to protect her tiredness from comment, so she covers it up with trivialities."

"There you are," Mrs Tanner cried, "you see you understand us all. Naomi and me and little Roger."

"Oh, Roger!" John said, "he's not difficult surely."

"No, but you've won his confidence so quickly. What was all that about Gumbleducks."

"Oh, it's an imaginary race of little men with whiskers and top hats that his father made up for him."

"Ah!" Mrs Tanner put in, "he doesn't tell us things like that. I thought he'd forgotten his home, poor boy."

"I was interested," John remarked, "because he's really such a sensible boy. He lives in the present. No ties or fears. I thought I'd found a chink. But I was wrong. He was resentful when I brought it up. He knows that his life is here and now. The Gumbleducks are over."

Mrs Tanner sighed, "I'm afraid so," she said, "with those dreadful parents." She hoisted herself to her feet. "Time for my meal," she declared. "All the same," she said, "I'm right about love. We all need it but not too much. I was so interested when I read about Dr Johnson. He needed love so much—too much, of course, that's why he behaved so badly when poor Mrs Thrale married her Piozzi."

"You know your Johnson too?" John asked.

"Why shouldn't I?" Mrs Tanner asked laughing.

"No reason, I just haven't known many mothers. And

those I have didn't read much. My mother never read."

"She was probably far too busy. I used to be until all this illness and exile happened. But don't think I understand half of what I read. Only about people. Yes," she declared, "I can really judge people. After all, you know, I kept house for my father after mother died and headmasters of public schools entertain a wide range of people. And then Oliver was a very successful barrister. Oh, yes, I know the world. But not books. Do you know many lawyers?" she asked.

John took a moment to answer, "I'm so sorry," he said, "I thought I saw something creeping by the corner of the roof."

"The cat," Mrs Tanner said, a little nettled.

"No," John cried, "it's Roger. Heavens! his idea of spying."

Mrs Tanner looked towards the square two-storeyed Victorian house and there, spread flat against the purplish tiled roof, was Roger, shuffling his feet sideways along the guttering. He was dressed in an old coat of Jeremy's, its belt flying loose, and an old felt hat of Mrs Tanner's.

"Oh! he mustn't" she said, "those tiles are so loose."

"Well, don't call to him," John said, but he spoke too late.

"Roger!" she cried, "Roger! come down!"

The small head turned, displaying a large pair of dark glasses. "I don't know what you mean," he called, "I'm mending Mrs Tanner's roof. I've come in from Ludlow special to do it."

But Mrs Tanner was not playing. "Come down, Roger," she called sternly.

"Oh, all right! But I spied on you all the way to the meadow and you didn't see me."

"No," said John, "you're a first rate spy. But you'd better come down now. Mrs Tanner wants her lunch."

The boy began hastily to edge his way back to the corner of the roof above a derelict conservatory. Too hastily, for his foot wedged in the guttering and as he pulled at it to release himself, he threw his whole weight on to the rotting lead. It was the cracking of the guttering rather than Roger's scream that made Mrs Tanner retch. For a moment she saw him clinging batlike in the flapping black coat against the shining tiles, then something loosened and he fell down through the sunshine pool of glass beneath. For a second John stood trying in vain to distinguish the boy's screams from the crash of breaking glass, then he sprinted across the lawn.

When Mrs Tanner arrived panting, John seemed to be letting the small, stolid body roll back face down to the ground where it had fallen. "He's alive," he said and, not looking up, he turned the boy's face towards him and began to wipe the blood away. "He's unconscious. Concussion probably. He must have caught his head in falling. I daren't move him. I think a rib may be broken." He looked up at her, "Telephone for a doctor and an ambulance at once," he said. He seemed angry.

Mrs Tanner cursed her size as she tried to hurry to the house, but she welcomed relief from the nausea which the spattered blood in the greenhouse had brought upon her. When she returned from the house, John had slid his mackintosh and his coat under the boy, he had also

M

torn a sleeve from his shirt and had tied it in a bandage below the boy's elbow.

"The ambulance is coming from Ludlow, but it may not be here for twenty minutes," Mrs Tanner said. She produced a small bottle of brandy.

"No, no, no stimulants," John said impatiently. She lowered herself to the ground with difficulty. I've asked the hospital people to phone to his mother," she said wearily.

"Look," John said, disregarding the information, "you sit by him while I get a basin of water. Call me *if* he comes to." She could see nothing to do but hold Roger's hand, but every now and then she stroked the fair hair from his forehead. In a minute John was back with a bowl of warm water and a napkin. He began methodically to wipe the wounds in the boy's legs and arms.

"I daren't touch the bits of glass. In any case these cuts are not serious. There was a hæmorrhage of the arm but I've stopped that for the time being."

Mrs. Tanner said, "Thank God you were here." She stroked Roger's hand and gazed at his square little face, whiter now than John's. It was this whiteness that gradually made her panic. "Why doesn't the ambulance come?" she said, and then again, "they'll be too late I know they will. Oh they can't let him die, poor little Roger," she cried, "I shall never forgive myself if he dies."

John got up and stood over her, "Look," he said, "he is feeling no pain, that's the important thing. It doesn't matter if he does die."

For a moment she could find no words, then she said,

"How can you say that? He's a good, fine boy." Anger added to her growing hysteria, she began to weep.

"Yes," he said, "a very good, decent, ordinary boy. And with luck he'll grow up into the same sort of man. But there are millions of good, decent, ordinary men. It just *doesn't* matter,"

Mrs Tanner fought to hold back her tears. A moment later, she said appealingly, "You said that didn't you to help me? You thought it would help me."

John turned round from his kneeling position beside the boy's legs, "Good Heavens," he cried, "do you think this is a time to bother about helping *you*?" A minute later he turned round again, "I'm sorry," he said, "if the remark upset you, please think I said it to help or anything else you like."

It came to Mrs Tanner that she was alone with John Appleby; she got up slowly from the ground, "I'm going into the house to pack a small bag," she said urgently, "I shall go with the ambulance. I must be at the hospital to-night."

"Of course," John said and turned back to his task.

She hurried along the gravel path to the house and almost ran to the kitchen. Her panic died as she swallowed her dose of sugar. Such fears, of course, were entirely irrational.

Ten Minutes to Twelve

PALE shafts of winter sunshine lit up Lord Peacehaven's great walnut desk as he began to write;
before he had ended, the gentle melancholy of twilight
had driven the more acute sadness of the sunshine from
the room. On the desk stood an old fashioned brass
lamp with a smoke-grimy, dark green silk shade. He
snapped on the lamp switch irritably. He was a vast,
heavy man—too heavy it seemed even for the substantial
leather chair in which he sat. His head was square and
his neck bulged thickly over his stiff collar. His cheeks,
which should surely have been an apoplectic purple, were
pale from a life confined indoors. Across their flabby
pallor, however, ran little purple and blue veins that
recalled his former unhealthy flush. His grey moustache
was neatly clipped, but the thick white hair that fringed
his shining bald head was perhaps a shade too long.
Hairs, too, projected from the nostrils of his fleshy, pitted
nose. His green-brown eyes had a melancholy, anxious
look, but as he wrote they gleamed both with anger and
with bitter amusement. He muttered continuously the
words he was writing. The emotions his face expressed
seemed unsuitable to such an old and compact looking
man. Yet his pepper and salt rough tweed suit was neat
and cared for, his brown brogue shoes were brightly

polished. Now and again water collected at the corners of his eyelids and he wiped it away with a large Paisley silk handkerchief.

MEMORANDUM TO THE BOARD OF DIRECTORS OF HENRY BIGGS AND SON, he wrote at the top of his folio sheet of paper. And then after a pause, when he chuckled slightly—FROM THEIR CHAIRMAN. Then at the side of the paper he wrote in even larger letters TEN MINUTES TO TWELVE.

The following, he wrote on, are the *only* conditions on which I am prepared to continue to serve as Chairman. N.B. When I say the *only* conditions, the merest simpleton (supposing there to be any such on the Board and there most certainly are) may understand what I mean and will not, I trust, waste my time by sending me *alternative* conditions or any damn fool nonsense which I will not under any conditions entertain. (This means that they will go into the waste paper basket with all the other bumph that idiotic fools continue to bother me with.)

1. I am to have *sole* direction of Henry Biggs—the organisation which I *built up from nothing* in days before it was thought necessary for a pack of self-styled experts and interlopers to poke their noses into all sorts of business that does not concern them.

2. The direction of Henry Biggs is here intended to include any and every 'associated' or subsidiary firm whatsoever and wheresoever. (Subsidiary it should be clear to any fool means subordinate and the 'associated' firms only associated themselves because they were incapable of running their own businesses and knew that they

would make greater profits if they *were* subordinated to *me*.)

3. The organisation will revert to its original name of Henry Biggs and cease to be called Henry Biggs and Son. The incorporation of 'and Son' has only led to the interference of a lot of petty officials and jacks in office who have their own interest in mind and not that of the firm. Indeed it is probable that the whole 're-organisation' of the last years was engineered solely for that purpose and *not* as was stated in the interests of my son Walter. In any case the Son has being in and through the Father. This is an IMMUTABLE MORAL LAW and nothing to do with re-organisation for efficiency, being in line with the contemporary market, the wishes of foreign customers, satisfactory labour relations or any other canting claptrap.

4. Those who do not like the conditions *must quit*. I cannot undertake to run an organisation where burkers, shirkers and the rest of it are undermining confidence behind my back. I haven't time for such pettiness and if I had I shouldn't choose to use it that way.

5. *In any case* the following gentlemen will leave the organisation forthwith—Messrs Powlett, Rutherford, Greenacre, Barton (T. C.) and (R. L.), Timperley and Garstang. They are well aware that I have done everything possible to work with them and that only their own obstinacy has prevented it.

6. THERE MUST BE UNITY.

7. The Annual dividend will be declared on my sole responsibility. I will, of course, consult the accounting branch, but it must be clearly understood that they are *an advisory body not an executive power*.

8. The wage structure of the organisation will be decided by me and by me alone. I should like to place it on record that I have the highest opinion of Trade Unions and have worked excellently with them *when they have remembered that they are a British Institution*. I do not propose to deal with foreigners or with those who ape their ways. (No names, no pack-drill.)

9. Henry Biggs always dealt in perfect harmony with customers abroad within and without the Empire while I was in sole charge. Our customers respected us because we dealt with them in good faith and *stood no nonsense*. This practice *must be reverted to*. (They were perfectly satisfied with the tune we played until we started all this business of asking them whether they wanted to hear something else. From now on we shall play 'Rule Britannia' and they will like it.) If anybody doesn't understand what this means, it can be quite simply stated in a few words: Foreign branches and the Foreign Orders branch will stem as they should from the parent tree—that is to say MYSELF.

10. The watchword of the firm will henceforth be ACTION and plenty of it. The Orders for the day will be ACTION STATIONS. Henry Biggs is a living organism and organisms must be active (Keep your bowels open is an old and true saying). Shilly shallying, red tape, passing the buck and other practices of that sort will cease.

Staff Managers will concern themselves with what concerns them, i.e. canteen arrangements, sanitary conditions and the like. Sales Managers will concern themselves with *getting sales orders*. *The Board will meet for action*. Everything else must be left to THE MAN AT THE TOP.

These are the *only* conditions on which I will continue to act as Chairman. *An immediate Affirmative is absolutely necessary*. Look at the top of this memorandum and you will see TEN MINUTES TO TWELVE. That means the SANDS OF TIME ARE RUNNING OUT. (Any fool knows what 'wait and see' led to with that dangerous old woman Asquith.)

The old man read the memorandum through slowly, smiled to himself and signed neatly but with a concluding flourish; Peacehaven. He then shook a small Benares ware handbell. The door opened and a sadly smiling woman of thirty-five or so appeared. "I want you to see that this letter goes immediately, Miss Amherst," Lord Peacehaven said. He folded it, placed it in a long envelope, addressed the envelope "The Board of Directors. Henry Biggs" and handed it to the woman. "Certainly, Lord Peacehaven," she said. The old man looked suddenly tired and a little puzzled. "And, and," he hesitated in his speech, "I think I should like my breakfast."

Nurse Carver's high heels clicked along the parquet flooring of the upstairs landing. The panelling of the walls, the borad light oak staircase and the wooden railing always reminded ,her of a man-of-war in olden times. When she reached the large panelled lounge hall the whole family were assembled there, cocktail glasses in their hands, awaiting the summons to dinner.

Walter Biggs was standing, legs apart, warming his bottom before the red brick open log fire. His wife

Diana was crouched on the long low tapestried fireside seat. They both looked up at the sound of Nurse Carver's high heels.

Walter's lined red face showed petulance at the interruption. He knocked his pipe noisily against the fireside wall and said sharply, "Yes, nurse?"

Diana turned her swan neck towards him and frowned at his tone. She got up from the low seat, letting her lemon scarf drape around her waist and the crooks of her arms.

Old Lady Peacehaven, too, was stirred by the note in her son's voice. She sat forward on the sofa, hurriedly, slopping a little of her drink on her dove grey evening dress. Mopping it up with a little handkerchief, she said, "How is he this evening, Carvie?" Her voice was cracked and flat; the vowels more faintly common than Cockney.

"Ready for bed, I think, Lady Peacehaven," Nurse Carver answered, "when he's had his supper. He seemed a little agitated earlier this afternoon, but he's done his bit of writing and that's worked it off. I shall give him a sedative though at bedtime."

"Then I won't come up to say good-night," the old lady decided," it will only unsettle him."

Her younger son Roland's thin face twitched for a moment. He was seldom at home and he found so much there that made him want to snigger. He ran his hand over his face and through his greying fair hair, hoping that his mother had not noticed his flickering smile.

"This is the paper Lord Peacehaven wrote," Nurse Carver announced, holding out the long envelope.

N

"Yes, yes," Walter said irritably, "I imagine you can dispose of it though."

Nurse Carver's sad, sweet, somewhat genteel smile threatened for a moment to freeze, but she was acomplished at thawing. "Doctor Murdoch has asked for all Lord Peacehaven's writings to be kept Mr Biggs," she said, "he wants to show them to the new specialist he's bringing down next month."

"Oh, yes, Walter, I forgot to tell you. We're keeping all Henry's writings now." Lady Peacehaven announced it as though it were a new school rule about exercise books. Her plump body and heavy, old grey face looked more than ever 'comfortable' as she spoke and she stroked the grey silk of her dress complacently, but she looked for a second anxiously to Nurse Carver for support.

"Good Heavens," Walter said, "What on earth for?" He raised his eyebrows and his red forehead wrinkled up into the scurfy patches where his ginger hair was straggly and thinning. "Murdoch's had father's case for years. He knows everything about him. There's no possible point in fussing now unless he's trying to use the old man as a guinea pig."

Diana fussed again with her lemon scarf. Their daughter Patience looked up for a moment from *Anna Karenina* and stared at her father as though he had sneezed over her. Their son Geoff went on reading the evening paper, but he scowled over its pages.

"I'm sure Dr Murdoch would only do what's best for your father, wouldn't he, Carvie?" Lady Peacehaven said.

Before Nurse Carver could answer, Roland Biggs had turned towards his brother and said contemptuously,

"You love to throw around words like 'guinea pig' Walter, don't you? You've no knowledge of any branch of medicine any more than of any other science. At bottom you're as frightened as any primitive savage, but a bit of bluster helps to warm the cockles of your heart."

Walter laughed to reduce the level of his brother's words to schoolboy ragging, "A bio-chemist naturally understands every aspect of mental disease I suppose," he said, and when his brother gave no answer, his laughter ceased and he added aggressively, "Well, isn't that what you're trying to claim?" Roland hesitated for a moment whether to accept the challenge, then he said wearily, "No, no, Walter, only that a competent, modern business man knows nothing about anything."

"Now, Roland," his sister-in-law said, "you're being absurd. Lots of business men are very intelligent even if Walter isn't."

"Oh dear," Lady Peacehaven cried, "if I'd spoken to Henry like that . . . " She turned to Nurse Carver, "You'll join us to see the New Year in, won't you, Carvie?"

Now Nurse Carver allowed herself the pleasure of a genuine smile, "Unless you think I should be with the Finns and Sicilians. What do *you* think, Mr Briggs?" she asked Walter. He hesitated at her remark for a second before he smiled in return, but the teasing relation between them was an old one and therefore acceptable to him.

"You're reprieved from the kitchen New Year, Miss Carver," Roland said. He hoped to emphasise the fact that Walter appeared to take charge in their mother's house—or could one still say, their father's?

Diana gave her famous little mocking chuckle. "You're frightfully good for Walter, Carvie," she cried. "That was enchanting."

Her son Geoff turned his growl on her now rather than on the newspaper, "Why is it enchanting to attack Daddy?" he asked. A lock of black hair fell over his glasses, but the recession at the temples pointed to his father's balding pate. "Well," he continued quickly to prevent a remonstrance from his sister, "if I shouldn't say that, why is it enchanting to avoid a kitchen celebration? I should have thought it was just as clever. . ."

"I don't understand," Patience finally pulled herself out of Levin's harvesting and announced it, "I don't understand why there has to be a kitchen New Year. Couldn't they join us?"

"Oh, my dear," her grandmother said quickly, "they have their own ways—all sorts of foreign customs."

"I shouldn't have thought Finnish ways could be much like Sicilian ones," the girl insisted.

"You heard what your grandmother said, Patience," Walter was stern, "she knows best about it."

"I can't imagine anybody could know more about foreign servants than we do at Four Mile Farm."

"How true, how sadly true," Diana smiled across at her daughter. "You've only had Finns and Sicilians, dear mother-in-law"—Lady Peacehaven laughed dutifully as she always did when Diana addressed her so— "we have had Portuguese, Germans, Norwegians, Swiss, Belgians and—shall we ever forget her?—a Lapp as well."

"The Lapp," said Walter, "was jolly pretty."

Girolamo came to announce dinner and the company

rose. Diana and Lady Peacehaven led the way in intimate
laughter about the comic vagaries of foreign domestics.

Nurse Carver stood for a moment, looking at the great
Tudory lounge hall with her sad-sweet smile. Then she
sniffed, laid Lord Peacehaven's memorandum on the
refectory table and made her clicketing way up the broad
oak staircase.

After dinner they watched television for a short while.
Patience read on in *Anna Karenina*.

"She gets such a lot of television at home," Diana said
in apology to her mother-in-law.

"You speak as though I was ten, Mother, instead of
nearly seventeen," Patience said.

"I'm afraid my set isn't as good as yours." Lady
Peacehaven had strange notions of appeasement.

"I don't think its a question of sets, Mother," Walter
declared, "its more the programmes. They're designed for
a mass audience and you naturally tend to get the lowest
common multiple. On the whole, that is," he added
judicially. He was essentially balanced in his outlook.

"Ah," Roland cried delightedly, "I see we have a new
class now. There used to be those who had the tele and
those who were above it. Now we have those who have
the tele and are still above it. Good Walter, good."
Patience looked up at him from her corner for a moment
with interest. "I suppose," he went on and his tone was
now as judicial as his brother's, "that like anything else it
must be used discriminatingly." She returned to her book.

"Fisher the new history man organised some discussion groups last term," Geoff told them, "I said I
thought television was one of the chief reasons why

everything was so dead to-day. I mean it puts everybody on a level and nobody does anything about anything because they're all so used to just sitting and watching."

"They have such a lot of discussions at school nowadays, Mother," Diana said. Patience looked up once more in the hope that her mother might have spoken sarcastically, but she returned to her book disappointed.

Lady Peacehaven, however, was suddenly more than disappointed. Her fat, fallen cheeks, flushed pink. She got up and turned off the television.

There was an astonished silence for a moment, then Roland said, "So you think everything's dead to-day, do you Geoff?" Have you any conception of the progress that's being made in the world?" He turned on Walter. "It ought to be made a capital crime," he cried, "to give people a non-scientific education these days."

Geoff blushed red, but he glowered at his uncle and answered, "I don't think scientific progress . . ."

But Walter had had enough. "Why don't we play contract Mother?" he asked. "Geoff's even better at that than he is on the soapbox."

The card game left Roland to pace about the room. Finally he stopped before his niece. "Can you be persuaded for a moment to come out of your wallow in romantic adulteries and use your brain for a bit?" he asked. She looked up in surprise. "Come on. Play a game of chess." He sounded so like a disgruntled small boy that she burst into laughter and accepted his offer.

After some time Lady Peacehaven began to lose interest in the game of bridge. Despite Walter's pursed lips and Geoff's frown, she made desultory conversation.

Diana tried to answer politely without increasing the men's annoyance.

"Nineteen fifty-five has been a very good year on the whole, hasn't it Walter?" The old lady said, "considering that is how years can be these days." After a pause, she added, "Of course, we've got a sensible government and that makes a difference." Then to their horror, she said, "I wish so much I could tell Henry that we've got a proper Conservative majority now. But then he never knew that we had those dreadful Socialists, thank God." She sighed.

Walter seemed to feel that a comment was preferable to the charged silence. "I can't think what on earth need Murdoch has fussing about father's papers like that," he said testily.

Lady Peacehaven was quite sharp. "Henry's been very restless lately," she said, "sometimes Carvie's found him as much as she could manage. I'm only glad Dr Murdoch is keeping an eye on things. You don't want your father to have to go away again, Walter, I suppose."

Walter mumbled in reply, but once or twice again he returned to the charge during the game. "I wish Murdoch wouldn't interfere in the old man's affairs," he said. He seemed to feel that the doctor's interest was impertinent and indecent rather than medical.

"Things seem better in Russia from what I can read," Lady Peacehaven said, "of course, they're up one day and down the next."

"I've ceased to read the papers," Diana seemed gently to rebuke her mother-in-law, "they're so sensational."

Lady Peacehaven smiled a little patronisingly at her

daughter-in-law. "Oh, I think one ought always to keep abreast of the times, but then I suppose when you've been at the centre of things as I was in Henry's day. . . . The Geddeses made things hum," she added, but no one seemed to care. "Of course these wage claims are a bit disturbing," she told them, "but on the whole everyone seems very happy."

Their lack of response to public affairs came home to her at last. "When do you go to Switzerland, Diana?" she asked.

"At the end of next week," Diana replied. "We shall just get a fortnight before Geoff's term begins. This mild weather isn't very promising though."

"Saint Moritz used to be so much the place," Lady Peacehaven said, "but I never took you children. Henry was very much against people going abroad in winter, although, of course, he was very good when I had that attack of pneumonia in 1928. He took me all the way to Monte Carlo himself and travelled back the next day. The Blue Train it used to be."

"No Switzerland next year," Diana announced, glancing at Patience, "unless Geoff goes with some party. Patience and I will stay at the flat. It's high time she had a winter of London social life."

"Next winter," Patience's voice came from the corner of the room, "I shall be busy working for Oxford entrance."

"This is a game which demands concentration," her uncle said, "a thing that no humanist ever has." He frowned at his niece in mock sternness.

"Oh heavens," Diana cried, "don't give her any more

high sounding names. She's blue stocking enough as it
is. Neither of the children have *any* sense of humour."

Geoff said, "If Granny can attend to the game, I should
think you could, Mummy."

Walter said, "Now Geoff!"

While he was dummy, Walter got up and fussed around
the room. Finally, he picked up Lord Peacehaven's
memorandum. "You've no objection to my opening
this, have you, Mother?" he asked, and before she could
answer he had done so. Soon he began mumbling the
words of the Memorandum to himself and now nobody's
attention was really on the games.

Roland, on occasions, of course saw Lord Peacehaven,
but the old man seldom recognised his son for who he
was and, when he did, more often than not he remained
obstinately silent. Only in his memoranda, Roland was
given to understand, did he retain a kind of lucidity.
Diana never saw her father-in-law, on a plea, purely
evasive and generally accepted as such, that it would only
upset him. In fact, she disliked the idea of someone
closely related who did not know of her existence. To
the young people their grandfather was an alluring
mystery. Only Lady Peacehaven remained detached. In
her daily contact with her husband she lived as really in
the past as he did and this existence was not wholly
pleasure. But for all of them the memorandum was
secretly an intriguing affair.

"The old man seems to have slipped back," Walter
said crossly, "The last time he knew me properly, I'm
pretty sure I got it over to him that the firm had been
part of the Development Trust for years." He prided

himself on his capacity to reach his father's comprehending powers where no one else could.

"Poor old Timperley died last month," he said, "he
was invaluable to the firm in his day."

"Of course," the incredible thing is," he said, "that,
allowing for the extravagance of a lot of this, the old
man *did* run the firm almost as autocratically as he writes
here. He could, of course, in those days, but even before
I joined him, things were getting into a ghastly mess.
People just wouldn't stand for it. I well remember how we
lost three or four very big South American customers in
the crisis of '31 just because of the old man's attitudes."

"Labour relations!" he eclaimed, "I'd like to see some
of the men's faces to-day if they read this." And he began
suddenly to read the memorandum aloud from the
beginning.

"Really darling, I don't think this is quite the place. . ."
Diana began. But Roland turned on her angrily, "I think
I have as much right as Walter to hear what my father
has to say. Jacob had the blessing, you know, not Esau."

"I didn't mean you," Diana cried, but Lady Peacehaven's voice put an end to the discussion.

"I'm sure," she said quietly, "that there is no reason
for anyone not to hear what Henry has written. The
children are old enough," she looked in turn to Patience
and Geoff, "to appreciate that what their grandfather
writes doesn't come from his real self. He's sick in mind.
But we're not ashamed of his illness. It's a misfortune not
a disgrace." She smiled at Diana to show her that no one
attributed her attitude to ill intention only to ignorance.

Both Lady Peacehaven's sons seemed a little discomforted by her words; it almost appeared that Walter would not continue his reading. However their mother said, "Go on, Walter, we're waiting," and he felt obliged to continue. As he read Lady Peacehaven sat very quietly with her hands folded as she did when anyone insisted on hearing a 'talk' on the wireless.

When he had finished, Walter said, "I don't know. Nobody seems to realise the scope and the complication of business to-day. In father's day they could bludgeon their way through things. Nowadays it's like a sensitive precision instrument—the least faulty handling in one department and the effects may be felt right through the whole Trust. And the nation depends on it for survival," he added, in what should surely have been a proud manner, but came out in the same grumbling, whining voice as the rest.

Roland smiled, he could not believe in anything depending upon his brother. "What I find so distressing," he said, and his tone was genuinely sad, "is the awful note of anxiety and fear that runs right through that document. And I don't believe it's just because fathers' not in his right mind. I think that's what he must have always felt, with all his courage and individualism and high handedness. Of course," he went on, "their certainty was so limited. In fact it wasn't there. There was only a bottomless pit beneath their strength of will. I wonder how he would have managed in a world like ours where we pretty well know the answers—technical and scientific. It probably wouldn't have been any good, he would never have had the patience to wait for results, and that's the essential."

Diana handed her glass to her husband for a refill and began to rearrange her shawl preparatory to changing the subject, but she was too late, for Geoff burst out in a loud, excited voice:

"I think it's frightfully good what grandfather says. It's perfectly true we *do* want action. I mean a lot of us at school think that. And that about making things alive instead of flat and dull and having good reasons for doing nothing. I hate all those good reasons. I don't believe he's mad at all."

Patience sprang up from her chair. "Don't you? I do. It think it's appalling to write like that—ordering people about and demanding power for one self and never stopping to think properly. I hope I should always fight bullying like that whenever I met it. It's no better than Russia."

"Why shouldn't people be ordered about?" Geoff shouted, "if they get in the way and don't pull their weight. What's the good of being in charge if you don't give orders? Anyway it's not like Russia. You didn't listen properly. The whole point is that the firm's *English*. Grandfather said so."

"I know," Patience said. Her eyes were large with anger, "that's what's so shameful. Oh, I'm sorry, Granny, but it's made me feel so ashamed."

"I should hope so," Walter said sternly, "what an exhibition from both of you. You should *both* apologise to your grandmother."

"At least," said Roland, "it's brought the younger generation to life."

Diana looked horrified. "If it takes the words of some

one who isn't . . ." She stopped and put her hand on her mother-in-law's arm. "I'm sorry," she said.

"That's all right," Lady Peacehaven declared, "perhaps it wasn't a very good thing to read poor Henry's letter really. But I don't know. He always liked to raise an argument." She took up the pack of cards and began shuffling them, "Your grandfather had great drive, you know," she said to the young people, "and he worked so hard. He liked to do it all himself. He was very good to people when they fitted in with his ways. But I think Roland's right. He *was* always very anxious. He seemed to want to reassure himself that things were as he wanted them—no matter how well everything went. And he never relaxed or took a holiday. I used to go with you children," she spoke now to Walter and Roland, "to Angmering or Budleigh Salterton, but if he came down for a day that was as much as he could manage. One year, it must have been when you were still at St Stephens, Roland, some parents of a boy there, I think it must have been those Capels, suggested that we should go to Thorpeness, but we never did," she paused, realising her digression, "Your father used to ring up though, every evening. I don't think he felt convinced that I knew how to look after you. He *couldn't* let people do things their way. It was just the same when you grew up, it wasn't that he wasn't fond of you both, but he was shy and he couldn't believe you could manage on your own. Of course, it got worse, as time went on. I ought to have seen it really. I *did* make him go for a holiday. We went to Le Touquet and stayed at the Westminster. It was very comfortable although some people said we should

have stayed at the Hermitage. But Henry only stayed
three days. He started so many law suits then. He *knew*,
that right was on his side. And so it often was, but not
always. He got so angry sometimes that I could hardly
recognise him and moody too. His face seemed different.
Like someone changing in a dream. One minute it's
them and the next minute it's someone else. I think the
first time I really realised how ill he was came about
through that. It was New Year's Eve 1935." She
stopped and then said, "Perhaps I shouldn't tell it now,
but there's no sense in superstition. Henry was sent out
into the garden before midnight. You know—the
darkest man must come in with something green.
Although Henry was already turning very grey. But
when he came in again, I didn't recognise him for the
moment. It seemed as though someone else had been
substituted for him when he was outside. And soon
after that he had that terrible scene at the 'office'." She
put down the cards. "Well, this isn't at all a cheerful
sort of talk for a party evening," she said.

"No, indeed," Roland cried. He disliked personal
revelations. "Anyhow, now it is *really* ten minutes to
twelve. Where's Miss Carver?"

A moment later Nurse Carver came down the stairs.
"He's fast asleep," she said, "so I thought I might join
the merrymakers before I go off to bed myself." She
gazed at rather sombre faces. "Well now, Geoff" she
cried, "I don't know whether I ought still to call you
that. You're so much the man. The darkest man present
too. You'll have to go outside to bring the New Year
luck in."

Geoff jumped to his feet, "All right," he said, "I'll bring in 1956. You'll see. I'll make a it year of adventure and action."

Walter was about to stop him, but Lady Peacehaven said, "Don't be silly, Walter. Of course he can go."

There was silence when Geoff had left them. "He's the spit image of Lord Peacehaven, isn't he?" Nurse Carver cried, "perhaps *he'll* grow up to be quite a great man."

Diana shuddered. Patience came behind her mother and put her arms round her neck. She kissed her cheek.

Nurse Carver looked at the downcast features of the family with consternation. "Only a taste of champagne for me," she said to Walter in the brightest voice she could muster.